"I can't have children."

Susannah hadn't meant for the words to come out like that, so...stark and harsh. But she couldn't take his tenderness knowing how upset he would be with her keeping the truth from him. Turning away, she slipped her hands out of his and clasped them together in her lap. It took all of her strength not to run away.

Lucas stuttered. "Well now, you don't know that for sure—"

She prayed for strength as she continued. "I don't, but I believe that's the case. It's the only thing that makes sense. I know it was the same for, um, for two of my aunts. They were barren all their lives, you see, and I didn't think... Well, I believe that's the case for me. I can't—I can't have children." She choked on the words, squeezing her eyes shut. The words hurt so much to say out loud or quietly in her heart. "Lucas, if you want, I'll go. I know this isn't what you wanted out of our marriage. I'm sorry."

Annie Boone admits that sweet love stories are a passion. She also enjoys history, so writing about the two together is a perfect match. Adding spiritual elements reminds her of her own faith as she writes. Annie lives in Atlanta, Georgia, with her husband and the two most wonderful cats in the world. She loves to travel, cook for her family and friends, and watch as much sports as possible. Of course, she also loves to read.

COLORADO MATCHMAKER

VOL. 1

ANNIE BOONE

FEATURING: *Susannah and Lucas* & *Eleanor and Matthew*

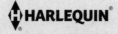

ISBN-13: 978-1-335-47409-4

Colorado Matchmaker Volume 1

Copyright © 2020 by Harlequin Books S.A.

Susannah and Lucas
First published in 2017 by Annie Boone. This edition published in 2020.
Copyright © 2017 by Annie Boone

Eleanor and Matthew
First published in 2017 by Annie Boone. This edition published in 2020.
Copyright © 2017 by Annie Boone

This edition published by arrangement with Harlequin Books S.A.

For questions and comments about the quality of this book,
please contact us at CustomerService@Harlequin.com.

Harlequin Enterprises ULC
22 Adelaide St. West, 40th Floor
Toronto, Ontario M5H 4E3, Canada
www.Harlequin.com

Printed in U.S.A.

Recycling programs
for this product may
not exist in your area.

CONTENTS

SUSANNAH AND LUCAS

Chapter One

Rocky Ridge, Colorado; 1882

Just like that, it was spring again. Snow still topped the caps of the mountains, but melted on its way down into the rivers. Flowers were beginning to bloom and the meadows once again looked lively.

No longer was the world white and grey, but filled with greens and almost all the colors of the rainbow. Even the air felt different. Susannah Jessup inhaled deeply and brushed her blond curls back over her shoulder.

"It's going to be a beautiful day," she announced, hearing footsteps behind her.

The door swung open and soon Lucas's hands were wrapped around her waist. His scruffy chin settled on her shoulder, a familiar and warm weight. Susannah couldn't help but smile.

"And so it shall be," he murmured, his voice still thick with sleep.

She touched his head, running her fingers through his coal black hair. "You're awake early today. Did I keep you up?"

A heavy sigh seeped out and she felt his shoulders slouch even further down. "It's all right."

His grip tightened around her waist and Susannah bit her tongue. It was her fault. Lately she was just so restless, and most nights she woke in the dark to stare at the ceiling. There was no reason for it, but there was just no peace to be found.

"I'm sorry," she apologized all the same and turned so that she could wrap her arms around him as well. The man was warm, and they still fit perfectly together after all this time. Susannah smiled, finding this comforting. "I'll try to be quieter."

His fingers moved gently up and down her spine, tracing imaginary circles that soothed the stress in her shoulders. They had been married for ten years now, and he never ceased to amaze her. Lucas always knew how to help her in one way or another, and it was always exactly what she needed. Closing her eyes, she gave him a tight squeeze before turning the two of them towards the door.

"Let's get some breakfast, shall we?" And with their arms around each other, they headed inside. Their cabin was spacious, one that had been made for a large family. Over the last five years, a second story had been added on top, and there were additions on the barn as well. It was 1882, and the Jessups had managed to turn their twenty acres in Rocky Ridge into a lovely home and boarding house.

The sun was barely peaking up over the horizon, and no one would interrupt the two of them for another hour or so. Besides, Susannah and Lucas liked the occasional quiet time together. Meeting each other's gaze, Lucas pulled out the flour as she brought out the bacon and eggs. Every Monday morning started like this, and it was a tradition they enjoyed.

"'Adown by the murmuring stream, that merrily winds through the valley, I wandered in days that are gone. With the joy of my heart'—Susie," he changed the name in the song at the last moment, making her grin. His voice was low and husky, his eyes dancing merrily.

"Shh," she tried to remind him, but he kept on singing, though a little softer now, as he came around and put his hand over hers, mixing the dough together. Around and around their hands went, and Susannah wondered how she could ever feel restless in a place like this. With a man like Lucas.

But deep down she knew why. And Susannah knew that Lucas knew as well. Ten years could be a long time, especially when it was just the two of them. Without a doubt, they had been happy for the time they had been together. Well, for the most part.

It had been six years ago when she realized they needed to face the truth. There was no reason to keep leading themselves on with false hope when the facts were set right before them. She would never bear a child.

After years of trying, it just wasn't going to happen. Susannah had felt the dread that afternoon, as though someone had officially told her. One instant there had been that vein of hope, and the next there was a cold, hard truth. It was a small whisper in the back of her mind, but she knew it to be true.

Chapter Two

Rocky Ridge, Colorado; 1876

Lucas walked in the door and immediately knew something was wrong. Taking his hat off, he dropped it and marched right over to her. Susannah could always meet that strong, steady gaze of his, but not this summer afternoon.

When they had first met, it was his eyes that had pulled her in. His eyes had convinced her to trust him and helped her to know she had been making the right decision to give him a chance. So when she didn't look at him when he walked through that door, he knew.

"What is it?" He demanded her attention, grabbing her. "What's happened? Are you all right? Did someone—"

Shaking her head furiously, Susannah ashamedly burst into tears. Hiding her face in her hands, she allowed him to lead her to a chair, and tried to gather her emotions. A grown woman, a woman with a lovely house and a wonderful husband, still wanted something more but couldn't have it. Though she'd tried to prepare these words all day long, now they failed her.

He asked several times over, "Something is clearly wrong, and I won't have it. Did someone hurt you? Who hurt you?" At first Lucas had been loud, ready to take charge and ride into the problem no matter what it might be. But then he grew softer, and knelt beside her. "Susannah, my darling, please. Let me help you."

Long blond tresses covered her face as she tried to hide her tears. It was one of her crowning achievements, the luxurious locks that she knew often caught the gaze of envious women. When it was completely unpinned, it went right past her hips. In the sun, it shined boldly like gold and she knew Lucas liked to run his hands through it. But this time, he was trying to push it out of the way, to reach her. The pounding in Susannah's heart only grew louder as she knew she couldn't put it off, that she couldn't lie.

"I'm sorry," she gulped, finally straightening up. Sniffling, she tried to wipe away the tears. There were too many, however, so she took to rubbing her face. Lucas grabbed her hands and pulled them away, bringing out his handkerchief.

He gave her such a look of gentleness that it made her want to burst into tears again. After all, he had no idea of what she was about to tell him. He couldn't possibly know just as she couldn't know how he would react. After all, the house had been built to ensure enough rooms for their future children.

Shaking her head, she forced herself to inhale, and motioned for him to sit down. Lucas did, but still leaned forward and took her hands in his. "Susannah, you can't do this to me," he tried to tell her delicately. "I just—"

"I can't have children."

She hadn't meant for the words to come out like that,

so…stark and harsh. But she couldn't take his tenderness knowing how upset he would be with her keeping the truth from him. Turning away, she slipped her hands out of his and clasped them together in her lap. It took all of her strength not to run away.

Lucas stuttered. "Well now, you don't know that for sure—"

She prayed for strength as she continued. "I don't, but I believe that's the case. It's the only thing that makes sense. I know it was the same for, um, for two of my aunts. They were barren all their lives, you see, and I didn't think…well, I believe that's the case for me. I can't—I can't have children." She choked on the words, squeezing her eyes shut. The words hurt so much to say out loud or quietly in her heart. "Lucas, if you want, I'll go. I know this isn't what you wanted out of our marriage. I'm sorry."

Of course, she wanted him to beg her to stay. She wanted to hear him say that she was being silly. She wanted to hear him say that not having children wasn't the end of the world. She wanted to hear him say he loved her no matter what.

But he didn't say anything and the silence lingered. Susannah's shoulders slumped as she buried her face in her hands again, and she prayed for guidance. Surely God wouldn't desert her, too.

But Lucas did. He silently stood up and left the kitchen, walking out through the back door. She didn't know it until she heard the door slam shut. The noise startled her and she jumped, finding herself alone.

When she realized he wasn't coming back, she wasn't sure what to do. It was late in the evening, well past suppertime and she was still alone in the house. She tried to go to bed, but sleep wouldn't come.

Each minute seemed like an hour as she tried to decide if she should stay or go. She couldn't bear the thought of never seeing Lucas again, but she may not be able to control that. She was certain he deserved a wife that was a complete woman. A woman who would bear his children and be the heart of their home and family.

But she couldn't be those things for him—or anyone else. As she paced the floor hoping her husband would come home and tell her everything would be fine, she knew it was likely that her marriage was over.

Now she had to decide if she should pack her things and go before he came home or wait to hear it from him that she should leave.

Chapter Three

Rocky Ridge, Colorado; 1882

Now, she shuddered and realized where she was. Years down the road, and Lucas was still there. Having noticed the ripple between her shoulder blades, Lucas squeezed her hand. "Susie, honey, what's wrong?"

It was such an innocent question, and she pondered why the answer had to be so heavy. She wished she could lie, but she couldn't do that to him. Not to Lucas. She had hurt him enough, and had sworn she would do everything in her power to make sure it never happened again.

But to bring it back up after they had been doing so well, her voice grew soft. "I was just thinking about... about if we'd had children. That's all."

He grew still. Stiffening, he took a deep breath and she listened, squeezing her eyes shut. She hated that so much, the way he paced himself like that. Lucas had been a Texas Ranger, and was now the sheriff of Rocky Ridge.

She'd seen him in action before, fast-paced and taking charge. But with her, he was different. And sometimes it scared her, wishing he would shout and yell instead of waiting to collect his thoughts. Any woman would appreciate that, Susannah knew, but sometimes she wished he'd let her see how he really felt. The raw emotions she knew were really there.

"They'd have your eyes," he said finally. "And your smile."

Her heart pattered. "Hopefully my hair, too." She glanced up at his. As usual, it was a dark mess standing up at all ends. She put a hand up to try to tame it. "I just don't understand why it's so unruly."

"It's the west, darling," he stated casually, having had all his life to get used to such a head of hair. "The wind does things to it." She snorted, since it's what he always claimed. "And we'd have four boys and two girls."

She tried to focus on the joy of that moment, and not on the loss of the past. After all, you can't miss what you never had. "Six children, really? That's a handful, Lucas."

He smirked. "You'd love it. You'd be running all over the place, trying to wipe mud off their faces. Half the summer those boys would run around so much we'd probably never even see them." She scoffed but he continued, softly swaying side to side with her. "And the girls would look just like you. They'd have long blond hair and the prettiest voices. Like angels, really, and I'd teach them to dance by having them stand on my boots."

Putting the bowl down, she sighed and reached up to touch his hair again. Mostly to straighten it, she told herself, but it also made her feel close to him as she watched his eyes. This morning they were more green than gray. The usual sparkle seemed dull now as he looked at her thoughtfully. "We'd go pick blackberries in the summer," she conceded to the fantasy, since she thought about it often herself. "And gather a little tree to decorate for Christmas. We'd swim in the river and have picnics every Sunday after church."

He nodded, still seeing something that wasn't there. "That would be nice, wouldn't it?"

And she looked away. "It would."

The moment came to an end as they both heard the trampling on the stairs. Every step squeaked and Lucas kept saying he meant to fix it, but they both knew it wouldn't happen. After all, it was convenient. It was the warning they needed to remind them that they were no longer alone in the house.

Pulling apart, Lucas started humming again and tended to the fireplace as she finished stirring the biscuit dough. Then sure enough, two seconds later Miss Lydia Cowell appeared in the doorway. The young woman was bright eyed and bushy tailed, her hands flitting about like a little bird's wings. She smiled brightly and then her cheeks turned bright red as she took a step back and bumped into the wall.

"My goodness," she proclaimed embarrassedly. "I apologize for interrupting anything. Shall I return upstairs?"

The hope in her eyes dimmed only for a moment until Susannah shook her head. "Of course not. Good morning, Miss Lydia. Please come in. I hope you're hungry. Breakfast will be ready any minute now, I assure you."

Skipping forward, she beamed and leaned on the table to look at what was cooking. Lydia Cowell was a young woman from New York City who had come west to Rocky Ridge hoping to find a husband.

So many other women—including Susannah, herself—had left homes in the east to find love and adventure in Colorado, Wyoming, and even as far as California. Back East it was like another arranged marriage, with mail order brides meeting their husbands just before the wedding.

The woman with Susannah and Lucas now was a lovely little thing with curly blond hair and bright blue eyes. She was short but her bold spirit made her seem taller. Still dressed in the latest fashions, it was nearly impossible to tell why such a slip of a girl would dream of being out in the open territory of Colorado.

But as she turned, the evidence presented itself. Her mother had been prone to fits of madness, and in Lydia's childhood the woman had thrown the little girl into the fire. Scars touched the base of where her left ear should have been, trailing down her shoulder and beneath the dress. From most angles, she appeared to be perfect and unblemished. But there was a side that her scars couldn't be hidden. They were horrific. Even Susannah had to remind herself not to stare.

"It smells just lovely. Are you in need of any assistance?" Lydia offered, pretending not to notice. Her eyes roamed over the table. "Oh, biscuits with bacon. Why, I haven't had that since…" she trailed off for a moment, as though remembering something sad. She shook her head gently as if she was refocusing her thoughts. "Well, I'd love to help if I'm not too late."

Lucas nodded, and handed over the bowl of fruit with a big smile. "Why, thank you. And since you're volunteering to help, I'd best finish preparing for the day."

His eyes drifted from the young woman over to his wife. Susannah met his gaze and they shared a sobering moment, glad to have each other. Her heart thudded and she knew his mind was working fast, just as it always did.

"I'll return soon, ladies." And with that, he left them to finish breakfast.

"He's very nice," Lydia announced once he was gone. She sorted through the blueberries and popped one in her mouth when she thought Susie wasn't looking. But Susannah always knew, and smiled as she pulled the biscuits out of the oven.

"And this is such a lovely home. I didn't really see it yesterday, seeing as it was rather dark when I arrived... I never dreamed that a land could be so vast. It seems like the trees will never end." She chattered happily as she picked through the berries, cutting a few of the larger ones before placing them in a bowl that she set aside.

The older woman nodded. "I have yet to see the end of it myself. But you're on your way to Nevada, and there's only more land to find after that." Everyone had heard the stories about California, of gold and the wide waters. They were supposed to be warmer and bluer than the east coast.

Lydia sighed, leaning against a chair. "Perhaps Nevada will be close to the ocean. If there's anything I miss about home, it would be the water. I know New York City doesn't have a festive waterfront, but Mrs. Jessup, I miss it even now."

Standing up, Susannah patted the girl's knee. "Perhaps your future husband will take you there. You never know."

It made the girl, barely nineteen years old, blush bright red. "I—I suppose he might," she stammered. Looking away, she stared at her fingers, already stained purple from the berries. But she hardly noticed, already lost in thought.

"Lydia?" Susannah frowned, and touched the young girl again. To her surprise, Lydia jumped. "Goodness! Lydia, what is it? Are you all right?"

Blinking, the girl nodded uncertainly. "Yes. Yes, I…oh brother. I apologize. My thoughts were carrying me away. I was only thinking that—no, I'm…oh, it's nonsense. I didn't mean to bother you, Mrs. Jessup—"

She shook her head. "Please, call me Susannah. And what's on your mind? To distract you that much, it must be of some importance."

Shrugging, the girl turned away and created a wide berth with the table between them. She stared at her feet, and slowly the doubt became apparent in her brow. Susannah remembered the letters just as Lydia opened her mouth.

"It's just that I'm worried… I'm afraid he won't want me. I could know how to do everything—cook, wash, read, clean, work hard—and still not find someone willing to take me." She motioned loosely to the side where her scars were visible. The worry that hung on her made her appear much too old.

"Well, I think you're wrong." Susannah cleared her throat. "And let me tell you why. Because in your first letter, do you remember what you told me? Lydia Cowell, you said you needed to find a home where freedom and God were present. You weren't even looking for love or an easy life which I am certain you could have found in New York. You said you wanted to find joy in whatever form it came in."

The girl smiled briefly, then looked away.

"That's why you're here. Because you're on your way to Nevada, where you are going to marry Mr. Joshua Ralph. Now, I personally know Joshua since he served in the Rangers with my husband." That garnered some attention and Susannah lifted her head proudly. "He lost his wife over three years ago, and refused to even consider anyone else. He refused until I brought you to his attention, that is."

Lydia paused, staring at her fingers. "Oh?" And she bit her lip. "Wh-what did he say?"

Chuckling, Susannah went over and grabbed the girl's hands. "He said that he didn't deserve such a strong woman, but would do anything he could to give you a good and happy home." And she watched as the light slowly returned to the girl's eyes.

She had hesitated on this match for a good while, knowing instantly that it was a good one but worried that no one else would agree. They were ten years apart and with a world of differences between them. There was something about the way Lydia had written to her, however, looking for anything that might be better than home. Better than New York, where people stared at her and whispered. Where they played up pretenses simply to hear about the horror she'd lived through. And better than how her father wouldn't look at her because his guilt wouldn't allow it.

Joshua was a good man, and needed joy in his life again. Susannah didn't have a single doubt that this would be a perfect match, and could hardly wait for

Joshua's arrival. Was it one week, she wondered, or two to go? That would depend on how his travels went.

"Do you think he'll stare?" Lydia asked softly.

Susannah sighed. "It's always possible. But I don't think it'll be in the way that you're thinking." The young woman looked up questioningly and she grinned. "You're a lovely young woman, and don't let anyone say otherwise. Joshua has no idea how fortunate he's about to become."

That garnered a small giggle. "You're too kind." She gave Susannah a cheerful look and it appeared as though she were about to say something else. But then she gasped and turned to the bacon in the skillet. "Oh dear! We don't want that to burn." And she hurried to help.

They worked side by side to finish putting breakfast together, and left off the heavy topics to allow for light chatter so their hands could keep working. As the bacon slices piled onto the platter, the other boarders slowly made their way down, creaking with every step. First there was Rosalie, and then Jane and Mary came down together. And the last one at the moment was Lorelai, quiet as a mouse who slid into a seat and poured everyone some milk.

By the time Lucas returned to the kitchen, the six women were chattering happily around the table. Susannah, mostly listening, stood up and smiled at him. Any tension from earlier had disappeared as he quietly stepped over to sit across from her at the other end of the table. Conversation continued as though they never noticed he had arrived.

"Oh, you must," Rosalie was proclaiming loudly. "You simply must, before you go. It was two days ago when the pastor loaned out the appaloosa to me. His name is Smith, by the way, and I went right up to the first ledge in the mountains there. Oh, the air was so fresh and crisp, I could almost taste it. I'm sure if you ask, they'll let you go today." She glanced at Susannah.

The woman eyed the table with a raised eyebrow. "Not yet. Lorelai still has her lessons, and today Lydia and Mary are helping me in the garden. You have a train to catch, and Jane needs to practice her sewing."

Most of them made faces before bursting into giggles. Susannah's stern expression slipped into a smile as she glanced at Lucas who was fiddling with his food. He needed to be going, but he didn't want to be rude. It was always a quandary.

Since he would be taking Rosalie to the station, he had to wait for her and there was hardly a chance that the woman had packed. While he didn't mind stepping into a brawl in the street, any women he wasn't married to always made the man hesitate.

"I feel as though I'm back in school." Mary shook her head. "Who would have guessed it doesn't end once you're grown?"

It was a rhetorical question, but Susannah cleared her throat. "Because if you're going to live out in the west," she told them firmly, "then you need to be prepared. Just as you worked in the cities to know which streets to cross and when, and how to ride comfortably in carriages, it's important out here to be able to ride a horse, tend the land, and prepare to make the best out of the little you will most likely have."

Humbled, Mary glanced down and the other girls nodded, listening attentively. Though Susannah hadn't meant to deliver a lecture, she couldn't help it. She decided to continue since she was on a roll.

"It's important to me that if I'm helping you find a good man, that you're prepared to take care of him. I don't just allow any man to write and to find himself a wife, you know. If he's not up to my standards, then he will need to look elsewhere. I'm making solid, life-long matches here, and it's important that you uphold your end of the deal."

Lydia nodded hurriedly, always attentive and studious. "Of course. You know so much, Mrs. Jessup... and you're from the East yourself. How did you ever decide to become a matchmaker?" She phrased it with a giggle, inviting the other girls to grin.

"How did I decide?" Susannah's words faded away as she glanced up at Lucas. Their eyes met again, and she felt a tidal wave of emotions roll in. The last few years washed up all the pain and joy they had endured, the beginning of all their work in this endeavor. For a minute, they just gazed at one another, leaving the young ladies to glance between them curiously.

Finally, Susannah sighed and stared at her unfinished breakfast. They had time, she decided, for one more story if she kept it short and sweet.

"Well, it was a few years ago," she began carefully. "We found ourselves in a situation where we had a big house for just the two of us. We wanted to do some good for people who needed help. I'd played matchmaker for a few friends and found I was good at it. And the rest is history."

She smiled at each one around the table and her smile widened when she saw Lucas nodding his approval.

Chapter Four

Rocky Ridge, Colorado; 1876

In truth, Susannah's matchmaking started in the middle of where they had been in their life—settled well on the land and happily working together. Things were good, until Susannah came to the unsettling truth she shared with Lucas. Her firm belief that there was no chance they'd ever have children was shattering. When he'd walked out that day, she'd wondered if he would ever return.

The following evening, though, he returned from town as usual and brought home a new bag of flour, sunflower seeds, and honey. Along with several other provisions that weren't available in Rocky Ridge. That meant he had been to Colorado Springs, she knew, but he shared no details with her. In fact, he'd barely spoken to her at all.

He stopped in the kitchen and sliced off a hunk of bread from the loaf on the table and took it with him on the way to their bedroom.

Hmm, I guess he's not going to sit down with me for

a proper supper. Disappointed, she went to the kitchen and sliced some bread for herself. Spreading it with jam, she went back to sit in front of the fire to eat it.

She had letters to read from each of her two aunts along with a letter from Eleanor. Since Lucas had retired to their room without her, she decided now was the perfect time to open the letters and feel a connection with people who cared for her. She read her aunt's letters first. Both were short, sweet, and gossipy. Their quips made her smile and cheered her up for a moment.

Eleanor was an old friend from Boston, a place she hadn't seen in how many years now? They wrote to each other often, and it always sent a thrill through Susannah knowing that her childhood home was still very much the same.

"It's good to hear from you, Ellie," Susie murmured as she unfolded the pages, and began to read. Her eyes read over the lines one by one, and then over again. Eleanor had taken a trip to New York City, and had enjoyed her time but found little good company. It made her laugh. "Then you might as well come here. The company out here leaves something to be desired on many a day."

That was an idea. Susannah considered it as she read it over again. It grew more into an idea as she thought about her dear old friend, recently widowed and still struggling. She had gone to New York to look for better work, for a better anything.

Boston was the same, but things were hard for Eleanor. Familiarity wasn't the comfort it could be for her. It made Susannah's heart tight and she prayed to the Lord for His guidance.

Then, not wanting to go back to the bedroom yet,

she pulled out some paper and ink to begin writing her return to her friend. It was long work, penning a long letter like that. There was so much she wanted to say and her feelings just kept pouring out. But then as she came to the end of her thoughts, she realized she'd been writing for over an hour. For some reason, the letter didn't feel right.

So, Susannah had tossed it aside, and then cleaned up the supper that had been untouched. By then it was late but she returned to her chair in front of the fire, anxious to pen the right words.

The two of them had grown up as childhood friends, and had been as close as sisters for most of their lives. When Susannah felt the need to leave Boston, she came to Colorado for Lucas as his mail order bride. That had been a tearful goodbye, but they had felt certain they would see each other again in their lifetime.

The next thing Susannah knew was Lucas shaking her awake. She looked up and saw out the window that dawn was just breaking.

"What are you doing?" His words were gruff and his touch was impersonal. She was quickly reminded that they hadn't resolved their issues.

The paper she'd been writing on stuck to her cheek and she could see ink spotting her hands when she pulled it away. Sheepishly, she tried to straighten up and fluff her hair. Yawning, she stood up and glanced out the window.

"I was only—oh my, oh dear! What time is it? Honestly, I've only been resting my eyes…" Hurrying around the room, she tried to shuffle the papers back into their order, tucking the letter she had so recently finished under one arm and the opened letter in the other. "Let me get something over the fire now, before you leave—"

"No need," he interrupted, and picked up his hat. "I'll just get something in town."

She paused at the door and looked at him, stunned. He wouldn't even look back at her. He never ate in town. If anything, the man pronounced his extreme distaste for the despicable, cold food at Danny's. And it was Monday, their day for big fluffy biscuits. "Oh." It was all she could say. "Of course."

Her eyes drifted down to the letter, still partially written, and suddenly she felt the strong impulse to find some companionship. It had been years since she'd seen anyone from home or family. While her Aunt Ruby had stopped in Colorado while moving with her husband to Oregon, no one else had visited. It wasn't exactly easy, picking up and leaving for a trip across the country just for a visit, though, and she understood. Susannah slumped against the doorway, and considered her options.

Chapter Five

Rocky Ridge, Colorado; 1882

Lydia glanced around the table. Lucas had stopped eating, his fork resting on his plate. Even though Susannah wasn't saying anything about the trouble in their relationship, he still seemed nervous.

Lydia's hands cupped her chin and she sighed. "So, this means you started this because of your friend, Eleanor?"

Susannah smiled and nodded. "That was the first match I made." Then she sighed. She had just received a letter from her friend from not three days ago, sharing that she was preparing to give birth to her second child. Susie made a mental note to tell Lucas that they would need to take a short break from bringing in women so that they could go visit soon. She was anxious to get her hands on those two babies.

"And what did you think of it, Mr. Jessup?"

All eyes turned to him as he stopped a spoonful on the way to his mouth. He'd finally begun eating again and now they'd stopped him. Susannah held back a grin as he collected himself and shrugged. Things were good between them, and had been for years.

"I...well, Miss Eleanor is a nice woman, and Mr. Conner was settling down and searching for a wife. Susannah's always been good at seeing things that most people miss, so how could I keep her from bringing happy couples together?"

She nodded her gratitude and the other girls considered this. Lorelai, ever quiet, finally spoke up. "Was she your first boarder?"

"Not quite," Susannah said. "We took people now and again, folks passing through town who needed a place to stay for a short time. It was unofficial back then, but if the boarding house near the station was too full, then they were recommended to us. Trains fortunately only passed around the times Lucas was in town, so often he was bringing over guests that I had no idea we were about to house for a night or so. Eleanor, however, was planned and she stayed longer than anyone else at the time."

Chapter Six

Rocky Ridge, Colorado; 1876

After several days of tremendous unease in their household, as Susannah remembered it, she finally had her fill of the distance that grew ever wider between them. Lucas stepped quietly inside late one evening—much later than usual, in fact. He could still move around without being heard proving he still had skills that he'd learned as a Texas Ranger.

She'd been waiting on him to come home as she washed a cup in her suds bucket. Just her cup, since he still hadn't been eating at home. While food disappeared here and there, Lucas had yet to sit down with her for over a week.

After spending several days cooped up in the house on her own without any company but the animals, Susannah's patience had withered into dust. When she saw him sneaking around with a stack of blankets heading for the loft in the barn, she lost her temper.

Slamming the now clean cup on the table, she had whirled around. "You stop right there, Lucas Jessup!"

she demanded loudly, and pointed at him. The look on his face was guilty for only a second before he frowned. "I cannot take this…this silence. The coldness between us is unbearable and I won't take it anymore." Shaking the suds off her hands, she marched over to him.

Although he was taller, she didn't let his size intimidate her. "I told you about a problem I have—no, that we have—and it killed me to say those words out loud. You know I don't want it to be true either, Lucas. You know that more than anything. I'm just as hurt as you by this. But this is not the way a husband and wife handle problems. Sneaking around, not talking to each other, not sharing how they feel about something really bad that's happened. This happened to me, too. Not just you."

She looked at him with unwavering fire in her eyes. She was angry and hurt. If he couldn't see that, he was blind. Instead of responding to what she'd said, he turned to face her with a scowl and placed the stack of blankets he carried on a chair by the door. Then he put his hands on his hips. And finally, he finally looked her in the eyes for the first time in about a week.

They stood silently looking at each other, neither backing down. Still, Susannah's husband remained silent.

"Lucas, I understand you need to figure out how to deal with your feelings about this. Seeing as I'm doing the same thing, there are limits to what I'm willing to take. You have to treat me like I matter. My feelings matter, too. So, if you don't care about my feelings or if you've decided you don't want me anymore," her voice cracked but she refused to stop, "just be man enough to say so. Then I'll take my leave."

She put it out there again, waiting for him to take it. It's all he had to do. She wouldn't move until he said it.

Shaking in her boots, she had waited for a solid minute, waiting for him to say something. Anything, she begged, just anything. But it was true she wouldn't take his silence and avoidance another minute.

At night she had been hardly resting and the work around the house was more than shoddy since she couldn't focus or pay attention. It was making her miserable, and she had told herself a long time ago that she wouldn't live a life where there was more silence than conversation, more unsaid feelings than said.

But Lucas didn't say anything right then, biding his time as he gave her a measuring look. A good part of her expected him to walk out, to just walk away and never return. That's when the cold fear set in, raising the hairs on the back of her neck. He could really just be gone, and leave her everything. Why, that was worse than kicking her out. That would mean he was willing to walk away from everything just to have her out of his life.

"You're right," the words came out in the quietest whisper, so soft that at first she thought she was hearing things. Lucas's lips hadn't even moved. "I am… having a difficult time." He glanced away. "Susannah, I—we made a deal, a promise at the altar. For better or for worse, we said. I'm willing to keep it, but… I need more time."

It wasn't much better and her throat grew tight. Time? He needed time when she felt like falling apart? "I, um, I don't suppose I have a choice but to give you what you want. But how long? How much time?"

He shrugged, exhausted. Only then did Susie realize he wasn't sleeping well either. Part of her wanted to take comfort in that, but she could only blame herself. It wasn't what newlyweds thought of, after all, the troubles that came after making promises of love. "I don't know, Susie, I don't know. But I'm going to bed now."

"In the loft?" Her eyes trailed down to the blankets he'd left on the chair.

The man nodded firmly. "In the loft."

She had no choice but to let him go. Already she was dreading going back to their bed knowing that once again she would be alone. Those blankets would swallow her whole. "At least," she stammered for a compromise, "...at least come in to eat, would you? I—I can't stand to have you eating at Danny's this much. I certainly don't want you to starve. Please?"

"I'll think about it. I have a few chores to do." And then he walked out before she could say anything else. Her eyes followed his dark figure as he walked the well-trodden trail to the barn where he disappeared inside.

"A small victory," she said proudly, though she still felt miserable and lonely. "I'm sure he'll reconsider and come back in to eat something. The man does like to eat, after all."

But she was wrong, and he didn't come back in. Long after the food had grown cold, she stood out on the porch as she watched Lucas right outside their barn, chopping firewood. Dressed in yellow, she knew that Lucas had seen her. They were close enough that she'd seen his head rise up only to fall back down and start gathering what he'd cut. So she waited longer. But when he finished, Lucas headed back into the barn. Five minutes later, he still hadn't come out and his message was clear.

That evening, Susannah sat at the kitchen table by

herself, glancing at the empty place setting beside her. Silence rang out, and she drummed her fingers across her lap, only a whisper on the cloth. What had she expected? It was unnerving and she finally she decided that she wasn't hungry even at the delay in supper.

She put everything away, and sat down to read. Though Lucas had yet to return by her side for their nightly reading of poetry and the Bible, she kept it up. Just in case, Susannah had thought to herself, just in case.

She prayed that the next day would bring a change in her husband. A good change.

Chapter Seven

Rocky Ridge, Colorado; 1882

"That's it?" Lydia cocked her head and looked back and forth between Lucas and Susannah. The other girls shifted uncomfortably in their seats, food in their belly and a whole day ahead of them. By now the food was cold, and the story had the option to turn in two different ways.

Catching Lucas's eye, Susannah plastered a smile on her face. "We went to church and she met the town. Within a couple of months, or maybe it was weeks, Eleanor had met Mr. Conner, they were talking, and then married. They're still within a two-day ride, fortunately, and they're expecting the birth of their second child any day now." Lucas's eyebrow raised and she nodded with a smile. Standing up, she picked up her plate. "Now, let's get the day started, shall we? No need to be wasting any more of this beautiful morning."

As she took her things over to the sink by the window, she heard the sound of the other chairs scraping back as well, everyone beginning to pick up plates and shuffle to the kitchen. Her thoughts followed the trail they had been on as the young ladies began chattering back and forth. As always, as one of them left, they had fond words and tears to share before Lucas headed into town for the day.

He didn't go in every day, but most days he did. Rocky Ridge was a decent place with good people and there seldom were problems. He felt it was important to make his presence known even if it wasn't completely necessary every day.

Every year more people came to the valley and set-tled, building comfortable homes and farming the land. There were a few ranches with cattle outside the town and the range only widened from there. While there was occasionally trouble, Lucas was always prepared. He took his position seriously to ensure peace and lawful-ness. Rarely was he gone every day, and rarer was he gone for the evenings.

He could read her mind. Lucas's hand slipped over hers, tugging her from the dishes. Gasping lightly, she tried to hold back her wet hands covered in suds, but then he had his arms around her and they were twirl-ing in a circle. "Lucas, come on now—" she started to protest as the other girls giggled.

"Just one dance," he grinned, giving her a knowing look. It told her something and more, and she found herself reluctantly placing her hands in his. Soapy suds dripped down their arms, but he didn't notice as he twirled her once, twice, and three times before she made him stop. "Sorry for interrupting," he teased, both of them full well knowing he wasn't.

"Your turn," she teased him back, and danced one step back, forcing him to twirl. The girls laughed but he did so unabashedly, spinning another half to wrap his arms around her. At the close, they accepted the applause and Susannah shook her head at him. "Lucas, you're going to be late. The trains don't wait for people who aren't there on time these days."

The girls slowly pulled apart and Lucas left to saddle the horses. Susannah made sure Lydia knew where everything belonged in the kitchen, and then hastened up the stairs to Rosalie who needed to finish packing.

When she arrived, however, Rosalie was already packed and dressed with her bonnet on. Without anything to do, she was looking out the window thoughtfully. It was the same room Eleanor had used, Susannah recalled, and glanced at the young woman who was lost in thought.

Rosalie was feisty indeed, but it was something that had kept her going. Her father had passed away at the end of the war, and her mother had died of tuberculosis just a year later. Orphaned in Louisiana, Rosalie had struggled in odd jobs in a poor town before finding out about Susannah and the Mountainside Residence for Women.

Over the last few years, the Jessups had started the boarding house venture particularly for such women. It had started with Eleanor, and she had provided the idea soon after the wedding. Susannah had a way of matching people up, after all, and could help out other women in need. Truth be told, Susannah lived to help others find love. Her heart's desire was to see people happy together.

With time, it had turned into the Mountainside Residence for Women, where she helped women in need find proper husbands. She liked to think she helped families be born.

Rosalie had needed help, and had been there for just over a month already. That was usually the average amount of time for girls to be there, though it always varied. Her writing and reading had improved, and she'd learned valuable skills such as tending to the chickens and how to cook a good and nutritious meal.

Lucas had also taken it upon himself lately to start teaching the women who passed through more about wildlife. Adding that to the horse riding and caring for them, and he had a significant role in Susannah's operation.

After all, the Jessups wanted to help people. So they worked hard to ensure that the men they communicated with were good men who were prepared to build a family and care for them. They also worked with the women to make sure they were ready to take care of a family and a home.

Susannah was more than happy to have company, make friends, and even gain some help around the land. These days, they always had two or three girls there learning and working who would soon take a train out to meet their husband, or wait until their husband arrived to pick them up.

"How are you feeling?" Susannah knocked on the door lightly, making sure the other girl knew she was present. "Are all you packed?"

Rosalie turned around and grinned but her cheeks were tinged pink. "What? Oh, yes...yes, I'm packed and ready. I was just admiring the view one more time. You know, I didn't grow up around animals. I'll miss them, I think."

The reluctance in her face was something Susannah saw often, and her heart went out to her. It was always hard saying goodbye, even if their future was unfolding before them.

Crossing the room, she took the girl in her arms. "Don't you worry, Rosie. In a month, you won't even remember us."

She heard a sniffle as the girl hugged her in return. "I don't know about that. Why, I haven't had anything like this in years. It was nearly like having a family again."

Pulling away, Susannah took one of the girl's hands. Rosalie was soft and while she wouldn't be considered the prettiest on the block, the young woman had such strength to her that she could do anything she wanted.

It was one of the reasons that Susannah had decided to send her to Montana, to Carson Highling. The man had passed through Colorado only a few years ago for the health of his newborn child, having just lost his wife. They needed a new start and now he was looking for a wife. Rosalie did well with children, and would love the mountains there.

"Rosie, I promise you, I wouldn't let you leave my side without knowing that you are going onto something better. Carson and little Callie are going to be there the moment you step off that train and I promise, you're going to build that family you have been praying for."

The girl sniffed and wiped away a tear with her free hand. "You think so?"

Susannah shook her head. "I know so. Now, let's get this adventure of yours started, shall we? We don't want you missing that train."

Laughing, the girl grinned. "That's beyond fashionably late, I'm afraid. And if I'm getting married later this week, I want to know that man as soon as I can. You don't think he'll have chickens, would he? Or at least a cow?"

After picking up her bag, they headed downstairs to the porch. "He has those and possibly more. He's only got twenty acres now, but last I heard, he's working hard to increase his holdings. Now, be sure to give Carson our best, and here's something to keep you going." She brought out a small tin box filled to the lid with cookies. "Be sure to save some of them for your wedding supper, you hear?"

The girl pouted but promised. Susannah walked with her down to the cart that Lucas had just brought forward, but Rosalie paused before climbing up. "Well I'm going to be a married woman before I know it," the raven-haired orphan proclaimed proudly. "So do you have any last bit of advice for such a girl?"

She could feel Lucas's eyes on her as well, probably grinning. No, rather, she knew he was grinning without even looking at him. After all, it was a silly old story of theirs the day after their wedding when she had recounted embarrassedly all the advice she'd been given about becoming a mail order bride.

Chapter Eight

Rocky Ridge, Colorado; 1872

It was her two aunts who had provided most of the advice, with a few words from her mother as well. Her father barely said a word when she had been on her way out the door. While Susannah had been raised to be a God-fearing child in the city, she'd endured enough trouble there that she wanted to find a new life. A life away from the city.

"What are you thinking?" Lucas had ventured, stepping out onto the porch where she was standing. Susannah was still coming to grips with being in a new place. A new place as the wife of a man she barely knew.

She had jumped at the sound of his voice, and blushed bright red. "Oh, my," Susannah had stammered, and wrapped her arms around herself. "I didn't hear you come out. Is everything all right?"

He gave her an odd look. "You've asked me if everything is all right five times today. While my answer still remains the same, I'm rather concerned that yours might vary."

The man hesitated, while she was pondering his honesty. But that's what she had liked about Lucas from the beginning. He believed in keeping his word and stating the truth. The city wasn't like that, not one bit.

Glancing down at her feet, Susannah had hesitated. "I was just thinking, that's all."

"About what?" He leaned against the railing beside her, looking around. His hair ruffled in the wind, and nearly drooped into his eyes. She noticed again how nice his eyes were, and how nice it was that he looked her in the eye. Everything was nice about him, Susannah had thought to herself. Except, of course, for that nasty bruise that had formed on his cheek.

Hesitantly, she bit the inside of her cheek, a bad habit. "Well, I…my aunt told me that, you know, it was my responsibility to make sure that…that everyone was fed. I made breakfast, but, I think the horses already had some grain before I went out there?"

"That's right." Lucas nodded. "I woke up early and tended to them. I still have responsibilities here, too, and I'll do what needs to be done."

It didn't make any sense. She shook her head, frowning as it dawned on her. "Oh, no. You were up before me? I didn't even hear you. I'm supposed to be up before you even—"

She was trying to find the words frantically, realizing she was already messing things up and she'd only been in the house for a day. But then Lucas took one of her hands, and encased it in his. Instantly she became still, her eyes wide as she waited for him to do something.

"I think your aunts might be good women, but they sound rather silly," he put plainly. "Don't listen to their advice, whatever they said. We both have responsibilities and we'll figure out how it all will work. You looked tired and, well, peaceful, this morning. So I fed the animals and I was happy to do it."

"And came back to bed without my noticing," she articulated carefully, not sure if she liked that. How could anyone be so quiet? Biting her lip, she glanced away. "I don't understand. I'm sorry, none of this makes any sense to me. They sounded so sure of how to be a wife, I don't…so I don't need to make a cake for every Sunday supper?"

The laugh escaped him before he could help it, and tugged her close. It made her breathless. But that wasn't so strange, she reminded herself, since they were husband and wife. "You can make all the cake you want. I like cake just fine." He grinned. "And while I definitely need the help around here, we'll work it out together. If you have any more of that advice, talk to me before getting yourself worried."

She had smiled sheepishly. "All right."

Chapter Nine

Rocky Ridge, Colorado; 1882

Susannah looked at Rosalie thoughtfully and tried to pull back the laughter that was fighting to escape. "Well," she said finally, "be honest with him and he'll be true to you. Relationships are built on trust and respect, Rosalie. And though you may feel overwhelmed on occasion, just take a deep breath and dance with him around the kitchen. It'll set all your worries aside." Glancing at Lucas, now she smiled. "Marriage isn't a game with an end in sight, after all. It's about making your way through this life together. Taking steps forward and back as one, come what may."

"Amen to that," he murmured softly as Rosalie settled down on the bench beside him.

"You really think he'll have a cow? Do you think I'll be able to name her?" The girl had already moved on from her first question and was thinking of her new life. "I can't believe it. I always wanted a baby, you know. And did you see the sketch Carson drew? Why,

I bet she's even more darling in person. I'll send you my own sketch," she added to Susannah.

Nodding, she stepped back to allow Lucas to start the horses. She noticed a spot of tension in his shoulders, and prayed for him to find ease in this journey. It was always touchy with the mention of a babe, she knew, but forced herself to carry on. "I'll be expecting one within the next month, Rosalie. Take care!" And she waved until they were down the road too far to be seen.

Once she dropped her arm, Susannah turned around and looked at the house. It was made of beautiful oak, and they'd even painted all of the shutters a pristine white. Most of the windows had flowers now with the sun shining so bright. Why, it was picture perfect, Susannah realized. She was blessed in so many ways.

"Funny how we tend to take things for granted," she sighed to herself. And just like that, she was lost in her memories again.

Chapter Ten

Rocky Ridge, Colorado; 1876

He didn't say a word to her at church, though he'd driven them all the way into town. But Lucas had certainly had the nerve to act cordial and friendly with everyone else. Susannah had fumed all the way home, torn between anger, frustration and despair.

No one noticed how quiet she was, and he didn't say anything at all on the way home. He never uttered a single word. Her cheeks flamed up as they arrived at the house and she climbed down before he dared to try and help her down. Neither of them wanted to touch each other now, even a glance was too much to bear.

Too upset for words, she stomped off. Even home brought her no respite now. They'd had a morning mist and she hadn't put away the clothes on the line. Around the trail she went, annoyed even more that they might be damp. But fortunately, only a few things had been dampened again. She grabbed a basket and began tearing down anything that felt mostly dry.

"Let's just act as though nothing has happened," she

scowled. "Let's just ignore each other shall we? Go to church, pretend to everyone else that all is well in the Jessup home. What a—"

"I see you still talk to yourself."

Gasping, she whirled around to find Lucas there, pushing his hat back on his head. Biting her lip, Susannah glanced around. How long had he been there, she wondered, and how much had he heard? The sun was setting behind her so she knew he couldn't see the flaming heat on her cheeks, but it didn't make her feel any better.

"I, well, yes. I do talk to myself. For company, mainly." She managed to speak after her breath returned and then felt just a little bolder. "Since I didn't think anyone was here with me. And since I have a great deal on my mind and not a soul to talk it through with. When did you arrive?"

He shrugged, and glanced at the baskets before her feet. Clearly, the man didn't want to say anything else, and was expecting her to keep speaking. But it only made her more exhausted. Swallowing, she nodded and glanced towards the light in the house. Her shoulders slumped and she wondered what she had done wrong.

Oh right, she recalled despondently, she couldn't have children. "I see," she said finally, and then turned back to the clothesline, ready to ignore him. She pulled down three shirts before he said anything.

"Perhaps I will join you for supper."

He seemed to wait for her to reply, but Susannah was too lost in her thoughts. Eventually, he headed inside and she returned to taking care of the laundry. The work, she hoped, would distract her enough from the trouble she had managed to pile onto herself.

Though the two of them had had a few squabbles before, this wasn't like anything she had faced with Lucas before. Besides the overly polite and necessary words, they were still hardly speaking. It became an uneasy balance and she hated watching her every step. He still slept in the loft, however, and had yet to join her for a meal.

One Sunday, Susannah completely forgot the time—and the day, really—when she glanced at her husband wearing one of his suits, and realized she had forgotten to brush her hair that morning. It was time to be leaving to church, but she was so distracted that her hair was still as messy as a bird's nest.

"I can wait," he mumbled as she looked around frantically.

But finally Susannah's shoulders slumped. "No, don't bother. I… I'll go next week. Tell Mrs. Higgins that I'm looking forward to testing her berry jam in a few weeks, would you? And…and I'll be here when you return." She offered a wane smile and started back to the house.

"Susannah," Lucas started, but she waved a hand in the air and he didn't bother continuing. He needed time, she reminded herself. He said he would keep his word but he needed time. So she would give it to him, as requested. All the time in the world would be his. Sighing, she listened to him head down the trail and made it up to the porch, suddenly feeling tired.

Every part of her body ached, a soreness that had been creeping in over the last couple of days. She hadn't noticed much as she had been trying to keep busy. Sighing, Susannah sat down and leaned against the railing, looking out around her. She would rest for just a moment, and enjoy the view.

From here, the view was a pretty one with the valley before them, just past the trail with a large river weaving through it. During the winter, it froze over and he'd surprised her by bringing skates home to try. They both struggled to learn but it had been fun. She didn't expect to continue the activity, though Lucas probably would.

At the thought of winter, she shivered. Sitting in the sun for a bit would do her good, she decided.

Her eyes closed, and the next thing she knew, something was pushing her about. Groaning, she wrapped her arms around herself to shield them from her, but then she heard Lucas. Had he returned early? Rubbing her eyes, she tried to collect her thoughts. How long had she been resting?

"What are you doing? I thought you were going to town? To church?" she stammered, her tongue feeling heavy.

"What's wrong?" Lucas demanded. "Tell me, Susannah."

But she didn't care for his tone, and frowned at him. He started to touch her again, but suddenly she wanted to be anywhere but before him. Who was he to ignore her until suddenly it mattered to him? He couldn't toy with people like that.

"Don't touch me," she snapped, and then cleared her throat. It wasn't supposed to come out that sharp. "I'm fine," Susannah said calmly, and shakily pulled herself to her feet. "I was just tired, that's all." She went inside, feeling his eyes on her.

The tired feeling clung to her bones over the following days, and she could feel herself slowing down. It confused Susannah, wondering why she was so exhausted. It made everything much harder to do, and all of her chores took twice as long. There wasn't time enough in the day to accomplish everything.

She noticed Lucas staying home a little more, taking care of the harder tasks. And when he did talk to her, he spoke to her differently. Not the way he used to, and not even in that masked polite manner he'd taken to recently.

"I can make supper tonight."

"I can do it." She had forced herself to remain calm. "There's no need for you to do anything to help."

He was smiling, but it wasn't real. Pretending, she knew, since she could still see the tension in his jaw. His lips tightened whenever he addressed her, and Susannah found herself endlessly frustrated with him the moment Lucas showed his face to her.

It was like he was reminding her how useless she was to him. "Don't bother yourself with the cows," he said when she got up in the mornings. "I can feed the chickens as well. Why don't you have a glass of milk?"

"It's our land, our animals." She had rushed to dress as he did, trying to beat him. It took all of her strength, however, and she had to lean against the bed post to catch her breath. "I do this every morning, and I can do it today. If you still need time, then you can have it in here."

He called out after her, but she practically sprinted to the barn. By Friday, however, it was taking all of her strength to fight him and his petty comments. The only reason she could find for him trying to take on more responsibilities, her responsibilities, was because he was preparing not to need her anymore.

If she didn't have any chores to do, Susannah realized, there was no reason for her to be there. It made her heart ache at the thought and she wondered again how she'd managed to get in this mess.

Friday morning, on her rush to the barn, she tripped and found the ground rushing up to meet her in an unfriendly fashion. There wasn't even time to shout before she tumbled, and all the fight went out of her. Susannah's breath was knocked from her body and the world went dark.

Chapter Eleven

Rocky Ridge, Colorado; 1882

"Mrs. Jessup?"

She jumped, hands to her bosom as she turned and found Lydia there on the porch. The young girl looked at her in concern, and Susannah realized she must have been calling her for some time. It was just so easy to get lost in her thoughts sometimes.

"I'm sorry, dear. What were you saying?" She lifted her skirts and headed up the steps to the house.

Lydia bit her lip. "Well, we're ready for you in the garden. But I think you had best tend to Jane first. She found her needlework but I'm afraid she poked herself and now she's bleeding."

"A needle stick? Is it a lot of blood?" Susannah stepped inside, leaving the door open for the girl to follow. It had always bothered her how some women tended to faint at the sight of blood. Here in the west, you didn't have time to faint and hope someone would catch you while also taking care of the problem. "Ah,

Jane." She pulled out a handkerchief as they reached the sitting room.

Jane loved sitting by the windows with all the golden brightness the sun bestowed. Rocky Ridge was different than Chicago, where the weather was often cloudy and gray. On her lap rested a stitched pattern, nearly finished but halted now as she cradled her hand. "I forgot my thimble," she mourned.

She had needed a thimble indeed. She'd managed to dig the needle in deep. Susannah shook her head in disbelief. Not only did Jane lack a dowry, but apparently she had been deemed too clumsy to be married off to anyone back home. Though she could cook anything, she lacked several other skills and had been here for a few weeks as Susannah worked to find her a suitor. Usually she waited until the girls already had someone in mind, but Jane had asked kindly and she had agreed.

"Your finger is completely covered in blood," Mary stated in awe. "You're going to ruin that dress, you know. And probably your needlework, too."

That got Susannah's attention. She gave the younger girl a stern look. "Fetch me a towel from the kitchen, Lydia, would you? Two of them, one damp and one dry. Immediately, please." Lydia ran off, and Jane whimpered. Taking a seat beside her, Susannah got a closer look. "Goodness, it might have even hit the bone. Now Jane, I thought I told you to use a light touch on this. Not like when you're kneading a bread loaf, but—"

"Yes, I know. That's too hard handed for delicate needlework." The girl nodded guiltily and looked away, clearly understanding the mistake she'd made. "I was so close to being finished, I thought I could go faster and, well, I got carried away. Can you please take it out?" The question came out as a whimper as the young woman struggled to keep her tears at bay.

After looking at the finger carefully, Susannah nodded and touched the needle. Jane jumped anxiously and gulped. "On three," she told the girl, knowing it might be rather painful. "One, two—" And she yanked.

"Ouch!" Jane blinked hard. Then Lydia was there with the towels, and Susannah calmed them down as they cleaned up the mess. Once Jane was bandaged up, she was invited to take a chair and bring her needlework out to the garden.

"Can we plant roses?" Lydia asked as Mary brought out the shovel and hoe. They walked past her pots of blue columbines, Susannah's favorite. Lucas always made sure she had enough of them. "I love the roses, especially the yellow ones. I hear there are some roses that bloom all year around, you know. Wouldn't that be beautiful? Roses all the time would be perfect."

Susannah chuckled and handed her a bonnet. "Put this on or the heat will get to you. And no roses right now. Once you can tell the weeds apart from the vegetables, then I will personally ensure you have rose seeds with you on your way out of here. But vegetables first. Your families will need to eat."

"Vegetables first." Lydia nodded and paused as they entered the gate. "Oh, it smells."

No matter how many times the girls were surprised by the smell of the soil mixed with manure, it made Susannah laugh and she tugged the girls along.

"You'd be surprised at what wonders manure can do for the soil and for your vegetables." She started in on her lesson, well-rehearsed by now. But even then, her mind wandered.

Chapter Twelve

Rocky Ridge, Colorado; 1876

Susannah had opened her eyes just as she was being lowered onto her bed. Heavy arms dropping to her side, she felt the world spinning but managed to recognize her husband's face. "Lucas?" she asked in confusion. "What…"

He paused and looked at her, an expression of genuine concern across his face. "Susannah?" She tried to sit up, but he put a hand to her shoulder. "No. You took quite a spill out there, so just lie back and rest."

"What spill? I fell?" She frowned, trying to make sense of this. She started to assess slowly. Her boots were on, and she was dressed. Why, it was still morning. What was she doing in bed? And why did her head hurt? It thudded as though someone were repeatedly smacking her with a plank. Groaning, she put a hand up to it and grimaced. "Did I milk the cows yet?"

Lucas scoffed. "Of course, you're thinking about the cows at a time like this. But you shouldn't. Don't worry about the cows. They're fine."

Feeling ill, Susannah reluctantly laid back down and closed her eyes tightly shut. She had to be dreaming, she realized, and this was some strange nightmare she was experiencing. If she could just wake herself up, all would be well. Especially her head.

"A time like this? I'm fine." But as she said those words, a cold chill clamped itself around her neck and she shivered hard, her muscles contracting painfully. "What, um, what has happened?" she stammered again as a blanket was put over her and tucked in around her. "No, I'm—no, don't do that. No, it's hot."

But Lucas ignored her by pushing her hands back down and beneath the covers. "You have a fever, and you fell hard out by the barn," he explained finally, his voice fading in and out. "You're sick, Susannah."

"Nonsense." She shook her head so hard that the cloth across her damp forehead fell off. Her eyes closed and someone put it back. "I'm just fine."

He said something more, but Susannah didn't hear it as the blackness dragged her down. Over the next few days, she tossed and turned beneath the covers. Her body ached, and she couldn't even drink broth. On the occasions that she woke up and was conscious, Lucas was often there with a fresh cloth and a cup of water.

A week later, she finally gathered the courage to sit up, and found herself alone. It was late evening, she surmised, and there was a piece of bread on the nightstand beside her. Though her stomach grumbled, Susannah lacked an appetite and looked around to get her bearings.

Taking a deep breath, she managed to lean across Lucas's side to his own nightstand, and picked up the book that had been lying there. Keats, she realized, and smiled softly. She hadn't read his poetry and had wondered where this book had gone. She'd brought it with her when she'd come to Colorado. Fortunately she had a lantern already burning there beside her, and she opened the book.

"Ah, she's up." It was only the second poem, and her eyelids were already drooping. Blinking hard, Susannah looked up to see Lucas there, smiling grimly. He took a couple of footsteps further into the room. "I've been worried about you."

"Me?" she echoed faintly.

He ignored it, grabbing the chair from the corner and sat down beside the bed. Lucas took a deep breath, and then noticed the plate with the bread on it. "Aren't you hungry?" He picked it up and set it on her lap. She stared at it dumbly, gripping the book with all her strength. There wasn't much of it, after all, and if Susannah loosened even one finger on the book she was certain it would fall and upset the plate.

"Darling, you haven't kept anything down in days." Lucas's voice grew worried and she turned to him sharply. "Please try to eat. Just a bite, please."

It was a quick turn and she winced as her head began to ache. "You haven't called me that in a while," Susannah managed, forced to put the book down and rub her temples. "And no, I'm not hungry."

She watched him hesitate, glancing at the plate and then at the book. "Susannah, you need to eat. If you're going to get better, you need to eat and get your strength up. At most, you've had a few sips of broth over the last couple of days, and… I don't think you were even eating well before this."

Scoffing, she turned away. "I'm just fine."

"No." Lucas's tone forced her to glance back at him. He grabbed one of her hands, and the other rested on her calf that was buried beneath all of their blankets. There were, she had just counted, at least five on top of her. It made her feel like she was under a pile of rocks. But Lucas wasn't done. "You are not fine. What do you think you're doing to yourself?"

Exasperated, Susannah huffed. "I'm not starving myself, Lucas, I'm just not hungry. And I've been eating…" She trailed off, trying to consider the several instances of late that would prove him wrong. But as she thought about this, she found merit to his words.

Stunned, she leaned against the wall and frowned. As she went through the last several days before her fall, a stark realization crept up. He was right, Susannah realized, and wondered how she had missed this. It was so obvious. Picking at her meals had left her tired and her body too exhausted to function normally. It had made her tired and sore and slow, which resulted in the fall.

She was stumped. How could she have been so irresponsible? Biting her tongue, she looked away from Lucas who was still giving her a stern look. As though he hadn't played a single part in this, as though he hadn't done anything wrong. "It's not like you care," she scowled finally. "I'll just bet you would have liked it if I just disappeared."

The words came out before she could help it, but she crossed her arms and slumped down, hoping he would go away. Lucas stood up sharply and hovered over the bed the moment she finished, his gaze indiscernible. "Don't you say that," he managed in a low voice. "Don't you dare."

Now it was too tempting. She felt an itch under her

skin and she scratched it. "Why not?" she shot back. Hastily climbing out of their bed, she threw her hands up and tried to push him away. "Then you'd be able to marry someone else—anyone else. Then you can have all the babies you want. You and—" but it was too much, and she felt herself falling even as her breath gave out on her.

Lucas was there, though, wrapping his strong arms around her. It was the closest thing she'd had to a hug or touch from him that she could remember far too long. Carrying her to the bed after her fall, Susannah determined, did not qualify. Gasping for breath, she clung to him as she tried to gather the strength in her legs again. But before she could, he had carefully set her back on the bed.

She scrambled to sit down, refusing to be babied after that outburst. And he couldn't just ignore her, as ill as she might have been. After all, she was recovering. "Don't you just—"

"Stop." His voice was only a whisper, but it was enough. More than enough.

She froze, her breath bated. Lucas never yelled at her and part of her dearly wished that he would. If only everything were out in the open. But now, she told herself, maybe it was.

So, she waited. Clearly Lucas was fighting with himself as his eyes looked everywhere but at her and his fists clenching over and over again.

After a minute, he appeared to find his voice. "Don't ever—don't you ever say that again, Susannah. Don't you ever… Do you hear me?" His breath was labored as he fought to keep control of his tone.

It was a dark, shadowed look on his face that made

her still. Her throat constricted and her heart hammered. Suddenly she was glad he didn't shout. "Yes," she managed meekly.

Taking a deep breath, Lucas grabbed her chin to make sure she was looking at him, but she couldn't have looked away if she tried. The look he was giving her was so intense, she didn't feel certain she would ever blink again. "I would never wish you ill, never in a million years. I told you I needed time. Time to come to terms with all this."

"I gave you time," she whispered in a small voice.

Hesitating, his gaze nearly wavered. "So, you did. I needed it. But I'm afraid that I ignored you too much, and that's my fault. It wasn't my intention to…to stop paying attention."

Tears filled her vision. "I'm not blind. I could see all of it. Every day."

For a minute he was silent, digesting his thoughts and her words. Too long, she decided, and knew there was at least a semblance of truth to what she had said. Susannah had hoped that he would deny it, but he valued honesty too much for that now.

"I married you, and I intend to keep every promise I made to you that day," he said finally. "I care for you, and I do love you." Susannah's breath caught but she forced herself to take a deep breath. "You are my wife, Susie darling, and you come first." The breath let out with that name. She'd missed hearing him say her name.

Slowly she nodded, his hand still gripping her chin. "I'm sorry," she said finally, and made sure she looked at him head on. It was for everything, she told him with her heart, for everything that had gone wrong.

"I'm sorry, too," he replied, and he meant it in the

same way. And then, the spell was broken and she managed to blink as watery tears reached the corners of her eyes. Lucas kissed her forehead and then sat back down, looking as tired as she felt. For a minute they were silent, recouping on what had just happened. Then he gestured lightly to the food. "You should eat."

"I'm not—" Susannah hesitated, reminded of where she was. Her cheeks turned pink in shame. Glancing down at her hands, she suddenly realized they looked so small and frail beneath all these blankets. She could feel it, too, the lost weight and how light she felt. It wasn't a good feeling, and she felt embarrassed. Looking at her lap, she sighed and realized he was right. "Will you read to me?"

That was a compromise he could live with. First, he made sure she had eaten half the bread before he began, wanting to make sure she was eating something. And then he read to her like they used to, while she finished the bread and drank her water. It was a quiet evening and she settled back in the blankets as he continued reading, only to fall asleep to the soothing timber of her husband's voice.

Chapter Thirteen

Rocky Ridge, Colorado; 1882

Strange what time could do, and the miracles it wrought. Susannah blinked and found herself in the present after her brief reminiscing, where Lydia was poking at a pumpkin. "It's awfully funny looking," she was saying. "Isn't it a bit, well, green?"

Susie snorted and looked at the girl. Mary giggled. "That tends to happen. We have different seeds out here than what is used in most of the east. But don't you worry, in a few months they'll be big as the cart and I'll be able to make several pies out of it."

That made the girl hopeful, but she paused immediately as the light glimmered in her eyes. "Do you think I'll be there that long?" she asked hesitantly, turning away.

By the sound of it, Lydia was already attached to being here. Sighing, Susannah sat back and wiped the sweat from her brow. Glancing around, she unbuttoned her sleeves at the wrists and rolled them back. It was warm enough already with the suns on their back, and she knew they would need a break soon.

"I do. Especially since Joshua is driving out here to see you next month."

Lydia whirled around, since they hadn't cleared up when exactly she would be leaving yet. They always tried to be careful about that sort of thing, to get the timing right so the girls weren't there forever but on their way to their new homes and husbands. Susannah grinned, deciding now was as good as any. They'd received his letter yesterday, but there hadn't been a decent time to tell her.

"Really?" she squeaked. "Already? Next month? He's coming to get me?"

The girl really liked her questions. Susannah chuckled. "Yes, he is. A neighbor of his is driving horses this way, and he's promised to help. They'll be coming once all the foals and fillies are strong enough. I'm assuming five weeks right now, that's when they'll arrive."

"Oh," Lydia sighed, patting the pumpkin absently. "So soon. It's so quick, why I'm stunned. There's so much to do!" She started to stand up but Susannah laughed and pulled her back down. "Where do we even begin? Will my dresses be fine enough for him?"

She hoped Joshua liked answering questions, and grinned. "You'll be wonderful for him, Miss Lydia, I assure you. And we begin right here, in the garden, ensuring you're ready to head out to Nevada with him. We had best be hurrying so you can learn everything you need to know, of course. Today is gardening, and tomorrow is riding a horse."

That caught the young girl's breath. "Oh, really? I'll ride one? On the back?"

Mary finally piped in, her focus in hoeing lessening with all of the chatter. "Of course on the back! Where else?" And it made Susannah laugh before the other girls joined in. For a few more minutes they worked, until she decided it was time for a break and to check on Jane with her stitching.

"All right." She stood and wiped the dirt from her dress. "Let's pause here. Tools on the porch. Come along ladies, let's find some lemonade, shall we?"

Cheering, the girls quickly obeyed and they hurried inside to find Jane with her work nearly finished. Lydia complimented her kindly as Lorelai brought out the lemonade and poured glasses for all of them.

Sighing, Lydia settled on the couch and shook her head. "It's just so pretty. My needlepoint is fine, but I never know what to do and so it always comes out crooked or just odd looking. If I have a pattern though, then it's all right. I just need the extra help," she chuckled.

"It is rather difficult coming up with something new." Jane wrinkled her nose. "But I think it's still easier than riding a horse! Honestly, I don't think I should even get close to one. I'm sure I'll find some way of knocking it over or getting kicked. I know that happens."

Susannah shook her head. "Nonsense, Jane. Foals are born weighing at least as much as you so one recently born could easily knock you right over." The girls giggled as she continued. "And as for getting kicked, that only happens when you don't pay attention to where you are when you're near a horse. Some people walk up behind a horse and are surprised when they get kicked. Which is rude, because we shouldn't creep up on people or animals. You need to respect a horse for all that they do for you."

Nodding, the younger girl grew thoughtful. "We'll ride them tomorrow? And I'll start to learn how to not be rude to a horse?"

She grinned. "You and Lydia will, yes. Lorelai already rides well."

"What about yourself? Won't you be teaching us?"

She laughed. "No, that will be Lucas. I'm afraid he's a much better teacher, and rider. Today he needs to be in town for a trial, and then tomorrow the horses. We have just two, but the pastor will loan Smith. After you learn to care for them, you'll ride them."

Jane set her needle down very carefully, and then her thimble. "Do you ever ride?"

She shrugged. "Yes, I'm just not very good, I'm afraid. I can tell you the basics, but they're the experts. My riding style, ladies, should not be emulated."

And that was putting it honestly. As much as she enjoyed riding, her favorite mare had died recently and she had yet to find another horse that had a steady enough gait to make her feel comfortable. When she and Lucas still wanted to take a ride together, often she was sitting in front of him on his stallion.

The girls accepted this, however, and continued in their discussion about horses. After a couple of minutes, she noticed the girls growing too comfortable in the shade, and stood up after finishing her glass. "All right, ladies. We still have another acre to tend to before the noonday meal. Finish your lemonade, and let's be going."

They shared a few playful groans, grudgingly obeying before heading back out. Fortunately, the enthusiasm for gardening returned and Susannah was facing questions left and right. Time quickly passed with the girls eagerly learning new skills. After eating, Susannah had them return once again to practice gardening without her guidance. Just for an hour or so, she told herself.

Besides, she had company to prepare for. "Jane." She peaked her head into the sun room. "How is your crocheting going now?" The girl sheepishly held up a clumsily crooked scarf. Or what it would be, if she added several more rows to make it wrap around a human neck. "Ah. You need to be tight, be firm with the yarn, dear. Every knot needs to know it has its place."

"Hmm," Jane mumbled at the vague instructions, but her brow furrowed in concentration.

Susannah hoped it was enough guidance and then headed down to the closet for blankets. With Rosalie gone, the room needed to be freshened up. Was there another woman on the way? It was hard to keep track sometimes, especially in the spring. Everyone wanted to travel after winter. Thinking back, she tried to consider who it might be as she fixed up the room.

Chapter Fourteen

Rocky Ridge, Colorado; 1876

"Do you know if you'll ever have had enough time? To think, that is?"

He turned on his side, propping his head on his hand and looking at her thoughtfully. She let hers slip down on the pillow, looking back at him through the moonlight. He was still as handsome as ever, Susie thought, and wondered if he still thought she was pretty. Lucas blinked. "What do you mean?"

She shifted, pulling the blankets up to her chin. "We can't be like this forever, that's what I mean. Will you ever be content with just us?"

He didn't know. It was obvious on his face. The moonlight shone down on him, brushing against his jawbone as she tried to reach that thoughtful gaze of his. And then just as she was about to give up, she felt his arm slip around her waist and pull her close. Susie's breath caught as she curled into him, her head on his chest.

Closing her eyes, Susannah tried to relax. They

hadn't been close in so long, and she'd missed it more than she'd realized until she felt his arms around her. Now, she was surrounded by him and could smell that earthy iron scent he exuded so often. It had been so long so she now tried to drink it all in. "We'll figure it out," Lucas murmured finally, a hand drifting through her hair. "Eventually."

Chapter Fifteen

Rocky Ridge, Colorado; 1882

"Perhaps it's Sylvia," Susannah decided a few minutes later as she finished tidying up the room. Standing at the doorway, she gave the space one more look over before nodding in satisfaction. Not a spot of dust to be found, everything clean. Rubbing her hands together, she took the old sheets downstairs with her to put in a pile for the next day's laundry.

After the bedding went in the basket, she turned to the desk. Sitting down, she pulled open the file folders of her matchmaking work and methodically sorted through the most recent correspondence. The letters were separated in three stacks.

Those that had come and gone, those who were in the middle of the process, and those who had just started contacting her. Just a few minutes later, she could see that Sylvia Cormeleson from Alabama would be here not this month but the next.

As she reviewed her calendar, the woman realized that they might have a few days, maybe even weeks, without any boarders. That is, Susannah pondered, if Jane found someone and if Lorelai was able to pick up on everything she needed to learn quickly enough.

Shuffling the papers and files together, they were placed carefully back into the desk drawer. It always worried her, sending the women too far away where they would be out of reach from her. She felt she was still responsible for them even then, being the one who had set the match. What if something didn't work out? There was always the chance that in spite of her efforts, a man could have been untruthful about his circumstances.

Usually she tried to keep them fairly close, around Colorado and Wyoming. That had been the intention at the very beginning, after all. But there were only so many eligible men who wanted a mail order bride that she could reach, so occasionally she did need to expand her search elsewhere.

"At least I know these men for sure," she reminded herself with a nod. "All is well for the moment."

"Talking to yourself again?"

There was a smile on her face before she turned to him. "What are you doing here?" Her hands went to her hips. "Was the town getting too dull for you? We weren't expecting you until nightfall."

"Just wanted to see my best girl again." Lucas walked over with his hat, jacket, and badge already put away. As he walked into the light her smile slipped into a frown. The man had a puffy eye, already turning all sorts of colors.

Her hand covered her mouth. "Goodness! Lucas! Whatever happened? Now come here and sit down. I'll get you something for that eye." She hurried to get a cloth and dampened it with cool water.

He shrugged and took a seat at the kitchen table. "It's not that bad." He shook his head slightly as she hovered over him.

"No wonder you're back early," she muttered as he offered her a lopsided grin. "You're not a young man anymore, Lucas, honestly. Whatever happened? You're supposed to keep the peace, not—"

A hand covered hers and he gestured for her to sit down. Patiently he waited for her to settle down before speaking. She knew she should be used to this happening, and she wondered every morning if he would come back safely, but every time he came home with a bruise or a scratch her heart still dropped.

"Just had some youngsters coming through headed to California," Lucas sighed. "They were getting fresh with some of the young ladies in town, the Higgins girls. Then they bet I couldn't wrestle any one of them so I did."

"Of course that was to keep the girls safe, yes?" She raised an eyebrow.

He nodded. "Of course, dear. I wrestled each and every one of them."

He started to laugh and then winced, touching his side. But Susannah crossed her arms, realizing that her husband had deliberately climbed into the way of trouble and had clearly done this to himself. As she gave him a look over, she realized his shirt was ripped and his pants were more than dirty. He was a filthy mess.

"I won, by the way," he volunteered when she didn't say anything.

"Are you sure about that?" She looked at him with more doubt.

Lucas gave her a grin again, and his split lip started

to bleed. Groaning, she stood up and pulled out her handkerchief. "You know you like patching me up," he muttered. "And you would have liked seeing me beat those boys. Why, I walloped one of them so well, he was crying by the time it was all over."

She gave him a reproving look. "I'm not sure that's what you would consider nice behavior."

He raised a finger. She was staring at the bloody knuckles, wondering how those would come into play for plain wrestling, when he spoke up in a calm manner.

"Susannah, you know I don't try to cause trouble. But these boys were asking for it, and they promised to keep by the station until their train came. We made a deal and they said they would keep to it because I won. And now the women in Rocky Ridge feel a little safer."

The man had a point, but she didn't like it. There was a small doubt that those youngsters wouldn't listen, so she prayed to the Lord for safety. "Fine," she muttered. "And how many were there?"

"Five."

She stared in disapproval, wondering if he was trying to get killed. "Really, Lucas?"

"Did I say five?" He gave an odd smile. "I think it was just three, actually. Then again, maybe it was just two…"

She walked off. "I'm going to get the girls to start supper." Shaking her head, Susannah suppressed a smile. That wasn't something she could let him see.

The pounding in her heart slowed down the further she got from him, and she prayed to the Lord again to protect her husband. He was a good man, and had been a great lawman in Texas, she knew. She'd known that from the first day they had met. In the small town, he didn't always get a chance to exercise his abilities and every now and then he felt the need to test them out. She understood this, but it didn't mean she liked it.

As expected, the girls were crowded around one another, laughing and poking each other with the crocheting needles. Susannah gave them one last minute of fun before rapping her knuckles firmly against the door and gave them a pointed look. "I won't always be around to remind you it's time to start on supper," she started. "Everyone's going to be helping bake tonight."

Jane's eyes brightened as Mary squealed. "Are we finally learning to make your pie?"

"Pie?" Lydia glanced at the other girls. "What sort of pie?"

Without answering, Susannah returned to the kitchen. She walked slower, motioning for the girls to trail after her as they excitedly told Lydia about the popular rhubarb and blackberry pie. "Why, she even wins awards for it," Jane proclaimed, clapping her hands. "And she already made us swear, absolutely swear, that we'd never ever share the recipe."

Now they were being dramatic. But there was no denying she liked the warmth in her heart as the girls quieted down and started paying close attention. Her eyes roamed for a moment, taking the scene in. Lucas had already wandered off, though she was fairly certain he'd taken to the bench out on the porch to enjoy the setting sun. That is, he'd better be there because she didn't want any blood in their bedroom.

"Mary, would you mind grabbing the preserves? And Lorelai, we're also going to need to be working on supper at the same time. Grab the largest pot and we'll have fish stew this evening. Lucas brought in a nice haul of fish from the river yesterday afternoon. Jane, grab the onions and tomatoes to go in it. Lydia, get the pans and utensils. I'll show you which ones, come here."

The women bustled about, only running into each other occasionally and slipping into giggles. It was a large kitchen, and Susannah silently thanked Lucas once again for it. He'd finished building the place just before he'd sent for her ten years ago, and there had been a few folks who criticized his desire for such a large house. They said he was vain. But it was nice, warm, and met their needs.

"What do we do?" Lydia's eager voice pulled Susannah before she could start into her daydreams again. Blinking, she found all the girls waiting anxiously around the table. The stew had been started, though rather hastily, and was over the fire. It was a good thing then, she'd picked the easiest meal for the evening. It would cook fast and be quite tasty.

Tying her apron around her waist, she joined them at the table with a grin. "Goodness, I'm not certain you're all ready just yet for this—"

"Yes we are!"

"Please!"

"Don't back out on us now."

"Teach us," Lydia whined. "Won't you, please?" She even pulled out a chair for her, but Susannah chuckled and put it back.

Glancing around, she pointed to the eggs, and picked up a bowl. "When you make this pie," she started out carefully, "it's important to begin with the end in mind, and every step along the way. Every stir matters, every touch, and every berry. Most recipes can handle some shifting about based on what you have on hand. A few more beans, a few less potatoes, or fresh herbs if you have them. But this pie, ladies, every step must be taken with great care."

The girls looked on and took in every word.

"The eggs, and the butter. Thirty strokes to the right, twenty to the left, and three times again until it's nice and fluffy."

Jane watched with a crease in her forehead, already memorizing the information like a proper cook. "But you don't want a fat pie crust, do you?"

The girls threw her a look to silence her, but Susannah shrugged. "Trust me, you'll consider every pie crust too thin after this. At least, that's what my grandmother used to tell me."

Lydia brightened. "So it's an old family secret recipe, then?"

She nodded. "Yes, from the streets of France, at least seven generations. So each of you, you're going to take good care of this, won't you? I won't have poor copies being made of this pie, ladies."

"We promise," they chorused, and dove right in. Soon all the bowls and spoons were being used, and it became a busy kitchen with supper on the side. It was loud with their conversation and laughter, skirts swishing and smiles on their faces. Susannah's heart was as light when Lucas came to join them.

Jane gasped. "Goodness gracious!"

The other girls stared as well, but Susannah only frowned. His lip was definitely swollen, and now he wouldn't be able to kiss her for at least two days. And for that eye of his, he must have taken the cold rag off of it much too soon because the purple discoloration was far darker than before.

Handing the bowl over to Jane, she wiped her hands on her apron and went to him to inspect. She didn't say anything as he let her touch him carefully, trying not to wince as she considered the swelling. "My, oh my," she said finally, but decided that enough had been said about his actions. Besides, he had been trying to do the right thing, even if he chose to be a little too creative about it. "Ladies, keep an eye on the berries." She shooed them back to their activity so she could focus on her husband.

After grabbing bowls of fish stew and biscuits with butter, they went to the only corner of the kitchen that wasn't being used for the pies. He lifted her up to sit on the counter, but then he winced and she realized she hadn't checked his ribs. Frowning, she gestured. "How bad is it? You haven't even changed your shirt, Lucas."

He smiled sheepishly. "I fell asleep on the porch."

"You're not as young as you once were." She looked up at the ceiling shaking her head. "Fighting scoundrels, saving damsels. You still need your naps in the shade."

"Now, now. Stop reminding me how old I'm getting to be." He stopped her with a wounded expression.

As he took a bite of his stew, she leaned forward and kissed the uninjured side of his forehead. Though she sat on the counter, he leaned against it and they became the same height. For a moment Susannah watched him, pressed against her leg as he scooped up more of the stew. When a small crumb rested on the corner of his lips, she impulsively leaned forward and kissed him there, wiping it away.

"What was that for?" His brow widened before glancing at the girls. They weren't even paying attention, too focused on sprinkling the right amount of sugar over the berries to notice they were in the room. Lucas and Susannah were usually on their best behavior for the girls, after all, and rarely even linked arms around each other. The dance in the kitchen was a rare event, though they'd all enjoyed the frivolity.

He was tired, she could see that. The man needed another nap, and a few nights of good sleep. Something pulled on her heartstrings, knowing that it could be her fault. Not only did they have more people coming and going in the house, but a few of them snored. And she knew that her own inability to sleep straight through the night often affected him as well. "I'm sorry," she said finally.

The man paused. "What for?"

Sighing, she shrugged and glanced around. "All of it, I suppose. It's not like this is what you planned for, is it? Ten years down the road, a house full of strange women taking over your kitchen, and a wife who can't sleep through the night."

"Mrs. Jessup! Is it time? I think it's time! Can we put the crust on now? Can we braid it?" Lydia hurried over with all of the other girls watching hopefully. Such bright-eyed women, eager for a small adventure like making pies.

Lucas chuckled as she gave him a sympathetic expression and hopped down. Leaving her food and husband in the corner, she fixed her apron and showed the girls how to do a different twisted weave than most pies. One by one they tried it out until the two pies were well covered, and then placed them in their little oven.

"Just from the smell, they're going to be delicious." Lucas finished his food and clapped for the ladies. "Well done."

They blushed politely and began to clean up the mess they had made. Lucas winked at Susannah before heading to their bedroom. Hopefully, she pondered, he would tend to those ribs of his. But she let it go, knowing he wasn't foolish enough not to clean himself up before bed, and turned back to the women.

"They smell amazing indeed. Let's finish cleaning up while the pies bake, shall we? They should be ready to eat before bed and if we're lucky, we can do our reading while they cool down."

Everyone bustled around obediently, cleaning and reading before the pies came out. Lydia, the only one who hadn't yet tasted the pie, moaned happily and they begged for seconds. Tomorrow, Susannah promised them, and they finished their reading.

They read the story of David and Goliath, with the girls wondering again about men they would be marrying. But this time around, they didn't ask Susannah and instead chose to dream and romanticize their upcoming marriages.

Chapter Sixteen

But which woman didn't dream about her future husband? Her wedding day? Allowing the girls to dream was part of the process.

She ushered them off to bed and blew out the candles before walking slowly to her own room. Carefully, Susannah pushed the door open and peeked inside to see Lucas there, sitting against the headboard, one hand over his ribs as he stared out the open window.

She had been too nervous, Susannah remembered, to romanticize about him too much in the beginning. Though there were dreams of the cowboys, all she heard about the west growing up was that it was a dangerous place, a hard place, and not a proper place for women.

They spoke of towns without churches and morals, of brawls and shoot outs, of saloons filled with indecent behavior. This was all between the romantic cowboy songs and poems, of course, but it was the uncertainties that had been pressed upon her the most towards the end.

"We might get one more snow fall," he spoke up finally, never looking her way.

It made her smile. She kept the door hinges well oiled, convinced that someday she could surprise him. But his instincts were too good for her still, and he was usually the only one who could pass by undetected. I'll give it another ten years, Susannah thought, and stepped through the doorway and closed the door behind her.

"Do you think so?" she mused and walked over to his side with the window. She looked around curiously, and sniffed the air, wondering how he could tell. "It's been so lovely."

"Too lovely." He nodded. "Yes, one more snow."

"And it won't be rain?" She raised her eyebrow at him as she closed the curtains. "You're quite certain, Lucas."

He patted the bedding beside him, inviting her over. She went, but scooted closer to pull away his hand and inspect the damage she had yet to see. The candlelight wasn't good, but there was an obvious large bruise forming. She wrinkled her nose and shook her head. There had been too many bruises to count over the years.

"I'm fine," Lucas told her while she brushed her fingers lightly around his skin. The man inhaled sharply, and gripped her hand. "You're rather cold, my dear."

Grudgingly she pulled away and got up to change into her nightgown. "We put out the fire sooner than usual. Or rather, the girls spent more time talking together."

It was his turn to give her a skeptical look. "And you didn't try to get them to bed?"

She shrugged. "They're just so excited and happy."

He frowned. "But you could have come in here sooner."

That made her smile and as she turned to face him.

Her heart skipped a beat as she saw that he was grinning back at her. Fixing the sleeves on her clothes, she lifted up the hem and climbed into the large bed beside him. "You have a good point."

"I always have a good point," he reminded her. But Susannah gave a stern look at his ribs and he groaned in annoyance. "Susannah, darling, I—"

"I know," she interrupted. "I know. You did it for a good reason. But because you chose this method, this is what happens. You'll pay the consequences. As usual."

He frowned. "What do you mean?"

She interrupted him again but this time with a kiss on the nose.

"Wait, you can do better than that..."

This was what she meant. Susannah kissed his lips, and though he welcomed it, a second later she could feel him pulling back after feeling the pressure on his puffy lip.

"Ah," he managed, trying not to show that it bothered him.

The man could certainly have his childish moments. Susannah snorted and slipped beneath the blankets. "Tomorrow morning, we'll wrap up those ribs of yours. Do you understand?" She blew out her candle though he was groaning again.

"I don't need anyone fussing over me," he said, and groaned again as he tried to get comfortable lying down. Immediately she gave him an extra pillow and stared him down until he took it, so he could be well propped up and comfortable enough to sleep. "Stop it," he muttered.

She couldn't help a laugh escape her lips. He always pouted once the thrill of the fight ended and he was left to succor his wounds. "Oh you keep us both young, Lucas. One way or another. But stop whining and let's get some sleep. Clearly you could use it."

"A man—," his voice cracked and then he quickly cleared his throat. "A man shouldn't have to put up with this kind of treatment from his woman," he repeated in a deeper voice.

Susannah yawned and squeezed his hand.

"Of course, you're right. But things don't always go as they should, do they? Good night, my love."

Then she turned over to her other side, letting him know she was ready for sleep. Still, she could feel him pouting and it made her smile. In moments like these she had too much fun with Lucas, though she knew in the morning there was a chance she might feel a little guilty. But only a little.

Chapter Seventeen

Boston, Massachusetts; 1872

It was overcast, as usual. Grim clouds covered the skies and the sun was hiding behind them. Turning in a circle, Susannah couldn't help but smile to herself. Boston was, in its own way, saying goodbye to her. The city was also ensuring she wouldn't miss it much. It had worried her that she might spend the day in tears, but the cloudy skies confirmed that she was doing the right thing.

Her mother came out of the house, a worn-down woman with big eyes brimming with tears. She held a handkerchief to her nose and the other arm wrapped around her middle, always near to catching another sickness. A tall woman, she was always hunched over trying to make herself smaller.

Susannah watched her draw closer with a mix of love and a sympathy she'd carried all her life for the woman who had raised her. She'd done her best, but her mother had struggled with just about everything along the way.

But her three aunts had come by often, always there

to help. If Susannah could have anything at that moment, it would be the warm hugs from all her aunts, right there and then. Though there were cozy letters for her to read and reread, it wasn't the same as smelling Martha's peppermint oils, laughing with Sally, and having Ruby's fresh bread for a snack.

"Are you all packed, then?"

Her hands clutched her bag tightly. Suddenly it felt so light, though she'd packed everything she could fit. It wasn't like she could take that much, for she knew it would be a different place, different home, a different way of life.

But now Susannah worried it wasn't enough, that she would be ill-prepared. "I think so," she managed a sheepish smile.

For a minute her father gazed at her, now that they were at eye level. The man's eyes misted over, and she knew it was the closest thing she would receive to a hug from him. Having grown up with a poor and rough family, the man had worked in a factory for his entire adult life. She suspected the later years of his childhood had been spent working hard, too.

Everything he did was rather mechanical, from the way he always sat on the first left pew in the church to the way he methodically cut up each piece of his meal before taking a bite. A hardworking man, he had taught her so many valuable lessons, and she wondered about the wisdom of leaving for another man's house.

"We don't want to be late," he said at last. "So, let's be going." Taking his wife's arm, the two of them led the way down the street, crunching through the snow. Only eight blocks from the station, they walked together in the gray afternoon. Susannah trailed behind, already own. She stepped inside the station, reminding herself this was what she wanted. They hadn't pushed her to this, it had been her choice.

That didn't change her shaking hands as she showed her ticket to the train master, and then took her seat. Resting the carpet bag in her lap, Susannah watched anxiously for the train and occasionally glanced over her shoulder as though her parents might come back for her. Nausea nearly overwhelmed her but that's when the train arrived, and she forced herself to step on board.

"I can do this," Susannah told herself firmly, and opened her bag to look for something to take her mind off her nervousness. Rifling through her belongings, soon the young woman found the small fold of letters. Smiling to herself, she thumbed through and found the most worn out one.

My Susannah,
I like the sound of that. Your letter brightened my day when it arrived. I was attempting to build the front door to my house, and put the nail in the wrong spot. You see, if you put it in wrong, you splinter the planks so they are spent and only good then for the fire. It was a nice cherry oak, and that was my last plank. I'm afraid the door will be mismatched now.

You asked about Rocky Ridge, and I can tell you it's smaller than Boston even though I've never been to Boston to know that firsthand. Our little town is hidden there in the valley and receives a wide load of snow every winter. But when blooms in springtime, it makes every day feel Easter. Colorado Springs sits in a little fur-

uncomfortable in her jacket and realizing her bag was not that light, after all.

Everything they needed was close, since they were located just a few streets over from Main Street. The factory was twelve blocks east, with their church building four blocks north. Susannah's school had been just another block from the church, and the train station was east of them.

It was exciting as it was terrifying, Susannah decided. The thumping of her heart was so hard, it nearly gave her a headache. All her life she'd had dreams about the big adventures and exciting stories, always certain she would have a lifetime filled with excitement.

But over the last couple of years, she'd watched all her friends getting married and having children. Many families were still struggling after the war between the states. In the midst of all this, Susannah had realized she probably wouldn't be traveling the world or saving children from harrowing exploits or becoming a princess.

And so it was this singular adventure that Susannah had realized she wanted. Just one journey, and one that would last her a lifetime. The western part of the country was always changing and growing, or so she read. A place filled with as many outlaws as fields of wheat and corn. More adventurers than mountains. She was wary, but there was a small inkling of hope that she just might have something special out there.

"Susannah?"

She bumped into her mother and blinked. "What? Oh, here already."

They had stopped, having arrived at the train station much faster than she expected. Glancing around at the wintery snow-covered buildings, her heart suddenly went still as she realized that she was about to say goodbye to her parents. Probably for good.

This was it.

"We're here," her father stated, and shoved his hands in his pockets. His eyes strayed, looking around. It made Susannah wonder what he was thinking. The man had never left Boston. Fifty years old, and he had never stepped outside the city. But then, neither had she. Not yet, anyway.

Nodding, she bit her lip and looked at her parents. They'd never been apart for more than a night or two and had no experience at all with farewells. "The train will be here in an hour," she said uselessly, as though none of them knew that.

Pointing towards the door, her mother nodded. "I think the ticket master will be right inside there. There should be a booth or a desk." She sniffed three times. "He'll stamp your ticket and give it back to you, because then you have to show it to the man on the train. What is he called again?"

Her husband looked at her blankly. "The conductor?"

Susannah thought that was the man who drove the train but her mother nodded hurriedly. "Yes, yes, that's the one. The conductor, I'm sure of it. He will check your ticket. You must have it with you at all times."

"Of course, Mother." The words came out automatically, her mind already spinning a hundred miles a minute. Soon she would be leaving Boston for good. Had she done everything that she needed to, said farewell to everyone she wanted to see? Did she have her ticket? Her hand slipped into her jacket pocket, and she pulled it out.

Mother sniffed as her father cleared his throat. "Well,

you had best be going. We'll take our leave so you can so you can get settled." He paused for a moment, loo ing her up and down. Susannah felt a tickle at the ba of her throat and an itch behind her eyes. Surely the had more time? "We don't want you late," he said. "S we'll go ahead and go." He turned to his wife.

The woman threw her bony arms around Susannal "Don't forget to wear your bonnet. And make him th pie, Susie, he'll like that. Watch out for the outlaws, hear they take to the trains and that could be danger ous. And you'll go to church, won't you?"

"Yes, Mother." For a moment she couldn't breath but she didn't mind. It was the closest her parents wou get to expressing their love, and it was more than s had expected. Part of her wanted to collapse in mother's arms and go home with them. That little h with their round table and that old faded rug she always tripping over.

With a shaky breath, she squeezed her mothe before the woman stepped back beside her hu Their eyes were misty with their hands hangin side, her mother holding onto that handkerch ded up and damp in her hand. Susannah looke memorizing their faces.

"I guess I should go, then." She picked again, reminded that it was rather heavy. W wards, she bumped into the archway. " won't you?" They waved and her mother though the woman could hardly read.

The lump in Susannah's throat only watched them turn and walk away. Lik not one where they were leaving the their only child, to make her way in

ther in the opposite direction, and is a much bigger town. Colorado is a nice change from Texas.

No, I didn't grow up in Texas. In fact, I grew up far north in Maine and wanted to see the world as a young man. I drifted towards Mexico but remained in Texas to join the Ranger crew with whom I stayed for many years. Now, I can say that I'm looking to find something better. I hope it's here, and I hope you want to settle into a town, too.

I ask for little, really. I want a woman who can cook and be happy here, someone to warm up and brighten this house I'm building. I'll do my best to provide whatever you may need. I will never be rich in the way of the world, but I hope to gain wealth in the way of the land. Write again if what I've written doesn't stop you.

Sincerely,
Lucas

That was the first letter that Lucas Jessup wrote to her, right after she'd answered his ad in *The Matrimonial Times*. He sounded nice, Susannah told herself again. Clever even, and perhaps wise. Leaning back in her seat, the young woman sighed and listened to the train tracks. Grudgingly she glanced out the window, and saw how fast they were going.

It nearly made her heart jump. Gracious! They really were flying!

Holding back a laugh, she covered her mouth to hide the big grin. Susannah felt her worries drop away for a minute, and realized that she truly was on an adventure after all.

Chapter Eighteen

Rocky Ridge, Colorado; 1882

Lucas healed up nicely as the young women learned how to create poultices and wrap bandages. Susannah was even certain her husband was beginning to enjoy the attention, especially since the girls were always asking him to tell stories about his Ranger adventures. He'd pull out that charming grin and start on something new.

"You're supposed to be getting rest," she'd interrupt.

"I will when I'm finished," he assured her, so Susannah stayed close. But she liked the stories, too, for he told them well. A knack for story-telling and a pretty face, that one. Shaking her head, it made her wonder about the truth of these stories.

Soon Mary and Lorelai left, and there were tearful goodbyes after each wedding as one headed to Denver, the other to Laramie. With only two ladies left behind, Susannah concentrated her efforts on them. They required more time than expected, with Jane too worried about her clumsiness to concentrate, and Lydia always asking questions.

"They just scare me," she mumbled while trying to fix her hair after retrieving four eggs from the chickens that morning. "I don't know what it is, but those little beaks, they just…" The young woman shuddered and Susannah held back a smile.

Trying not to say anything, Susannah's eyes drifted out to the pen with the chickens, knowing they should have had close to ten eggs. But she had watched, and seen the little animals scurrying after the young woman with a fervor. It had been more than difficult not laughing. Deciding to go easy on her, she decided to find the rest herself. "I'll go give them a good talking to," she promised her, winking at Jane who was busy kneading bread.

She couldn't find her boots by the door, so she pulled on her husband's which were too large but it had been done before. It wouldn't take long, after all, with the pen being so much closer than the barn. Fixing her apron, she lifted the heavy boots one at a time and staggered to the pen.

The chickens clucked but she talked to them in a friendly voice, and carefully kept them out of her way. After tightening her apron, she retrieved the last five eggs before returning to the house. It had only been an instant, five minutes at the most, but they already had a guest.

She heard his voice from the moment she stepped inside, already opening her mouth to say something. Glancing around, there was Jane in the hallway talking to the man, whoever it was, and Lydia in the kitchen.

Rather, it was Lydia hiding in the kitchen, plastered against a wall with her eyes squeezed shut. Susannah frowned, and hurriedly put the eggs away after taking off her husband's boots, and went to the young woman. "Lydia? What's wrong?"

"It's him." Her eyes opened wide. "It's him."

"Him, who?"

The girl bit her lip and watched anxiously as Susannah shuffled through all the possibilities for who it could be. It's not like anyone was chasing after the girl and there was nothing untoward about her past. Why the only one it could be was…patting her hair down, the woman hurried out to the hall where she found him.

Hands on her hips, she shook her head in disbelief. "Joshua Ralph! Why, I hardly recognize you. It's very good to see you, indeed." She allowed him to take her hand gently as he gave her a deep nod. He'd only been to the Jessup home once and that was when he was in town to attend their wedding. They hadn't seen each other since. Occasionally he wrote to the Jessups, and she had always worried for him, especially after the passing of his wife.

He grinned sheepishly. "Why, thank you. And you only grow prettier, I do believe. My apologies for coming so soon, I know I wasn't expected for another week, but I helped Mr. Wigs move his horses and the weather was so nice that he decided to move up the timeline before any late storms hit Utah."

That made sense. Susannah glanced at Jane who had her hands clasped as she had clearly been trying to act as host. It made her smile and she gave the girl a solid nod for doing so well. But before anything else could be said, Lucas came down the stairs.

"I knew I heard your voice!" The men shook hands eagerly and she saw a lot going unsaid between them.

So Susannah took Jane's hand, and they gave their leave to the men who headed out onto the porch to catch up.

Immediately the women returned to the kitchen where Lydia was twisting her hair and biting her lip. She seemed more nervous than the night she had arrived, shaking in her boots even as she'd tried to remain bright and friendly.

"Where did he go?" she asked them. "What did he say? Did he not want me? What's going to happen now?"

Susannah held up a hand. "What did I tell you about nerves, Lydia?"

A big gulp. "That nerves may come but it doesn't mean that we should allow them to and make us do anything we wouldn't normally do," she muttered, resigned. Closing her eyes, she took a deep breath and dropped her arms to her sides. "He sounds nice, I think?"

Jane giggled between them, finally grinning broadly. "He is very nice! He called me sweet when I offered him something to eat," she informed them.

Nodding, Susannah glanced around. "That was well done, Jane. Speaking of food, let's finish up those eggs and get them on the table. And the bacon, too." Jane headed off and she turned to the other girl still taking deep breaths. "Lydia, you are not bound to do anything you don't want to, do you understand that? Life never goes according to plan. Sometimes things happen early, or they happen late, and sometimes they don't happen at all. You adjust no matter what. Now we need to get busy. Finish the bread for Jane, would you?"

Chapter Nineteen

Hard work always clears the mind, Susannah told herself and watched Lydia run around to make herself busy. Sure enough, within minutes the crease in her forehead had disappeared and her shoulders were relaxed as she started singing along with Jane.

With the kitchen being cared for and the men talking, Susannah decided to return outside. Lucas had taken his boots, and without her boots around, she made the decision to pull off her stockings and head out barefoot.

Sticking to the path to avoid stickers and stones, the woman made her way to the barn to check on the animals. Lucas had risen late and she wasn't certain the cows had all been milked. Saturdays had the tendency of being slow for the Jessups, and she didn't mind that the chores happened late or in a different order.

It made her smile now to think that it would allow them to have some more fun in the afternoon since there was little else to do. Perhaps they'd even bake a cake. She'd have to ask the girls, but Susannah had a feeling they wouldn't mind.

It was a pleasant stroll to the barn, and the smell of

fresh hay was obvious as she stepped inside. Leaving a door open, she glanced around and went over to their three pigs. One was still young and small, and it grew noisy as she drew closer. The other two were large and lazy, lying down though she could see that they had been fed.

Fresh hay, full pigs, had Lucas done everything? Recounting the morning so far, Susannah wondered how he could have. She'd gotten up, dressed, braided her hair, and then walked out to the kitchen where Jane and Lydia had already been up. They'd started breakfast as Lydia was assigned to get the eggs…she shook her head.

After checking out everything just to be certain that her sweet husband hadn't missed anything, which he hadn't, Susannah headed back towards the house. Halfway down the trail, passing by her two Baily Sweet apple trees, she spotted the two men winding their way around the house. Lucas's arm was in the air, pointing out landmarks and motioning to the barn.

They stopped when they got closer to her. "When these trees are bearing, we have a hard time keeping up. They're practically too bountiful. We make preserves, pies, and whatever else Susannah can think of. We sell what we don't use to the mercantile. And standing between them is the most beautiful woman I've ever beheld." The words slipped off his tongue smoothly. She raised her eyebrow and wondered if they were too smooth. Lucas gave her a cheeky smile as Joshua chuckled.

"It surely sounds like you've settled down nicely," the man drawled, and scratched the scruff on his face. It looked like they must have gotten in early and he hadn't even had the time to shave. He could smell better, too, she suddenly realized. That sheepish smile of his told her that the man knew it, too.

The smile only grew on her face as she took her husband's hand, thinking back to their wedding day. Joshua had looked the same then, though his clothes had been dustier. "I'd like to think so, yes," she grinned. "When he's not trying to do everything, anyways." The man played innocent and raised his eyebrow. "Marriage is between two people. That means we take turns, and let each other—"

Lucas cut her off with a grin. "I think you're the only wife in the world who complains when her husband does all the work." Wrapping his arm around her, he kissed her softly on the top of her head. "You're welcome, by the way."

It just made Joshua smile, and she could see the thoughts in his eyes. He'd married while still with the Rangers, and he'd always had good things to say about his Elizabeth. But over three years ago, just after he had decided to leave that service for good, his wife had gone into early labor and neither she nor the babe had survived. He had waited nearly a year to write to them and tell them, and she knew it would have been hard.

What was it like, to truly be alone? Susannah realized she had never experienced that. Through the rough and tumble spots of her marriage, she had certainly felt the weight of the situation, but never had she been truly, thoroughly, alone.

But that's why he was here. And her smile widened, thinking of Lydia. Of bright, cheerful Lydia with that big smile and her soft hair. They would be perfect together, and she'd known it from the moment they had both written. Even Lucas had agreed it could work.

Now, she only needed to get the young woman to shake off her nerves.

How? To push them together, that could work, but Lydia was too good at getting flustered. Susannah shook her head. She'd figure it out. "Cake," she announced, and the men looked at her. "I thought we'd make a cake today. Joshua, I'm assuming you want to bathe and shave sometime today, and that you could return here for an early supper. What do you say?"

Lucas raised his eyebrow. "You can stay if you like, and we haven't even finished the tour." He gave his wife a questioning look on why the man couldn't just stay and relax but she only shrugged.

The other man shook his head. "Oh no, she's right. I'll be needing to return to town. I know this isn't what either of you could have expected, and I don't want to intrude. I can even wait another week before—"

Susannah interrupted as she waved her hand. "Of course not. You're returning this evening for supper, and we're all having cake for dessert. There's a chance someone might even pull out their fiddle."

Lucas groaned, and it made her and Joshua laugh. "That would be torture for everyone, I think we can agree." He shook his head in a grimace. "I haven't picked that thing up in months. You probably play better than me."

Susannah made a face. Though he had played a violin most of his life, it had come in last place as an adult. Once she had decided to ask him for lessons, but she had never realized how difficult it was to play and they were too impatient to continue them. Her smile grew at the two of them trying to catch each other off balance.

Odd man out, Joshua cleared his throat. "Four o'clock, then?"

"Four," Lucas and Susannah chimed in together. She pulled away and looked up at Lucas with a grin. "But you two should finish the tour. And talk about that new horse we've been considering," she added as an afterthought.

He raised an eyebrow. "Another one?"

Lucas nodded as she stepped away and headed towards the house. "Her horse took ill and…well, she hasn't found a new one with an easy gait. And we're thinking smaller, but one that can still climb the mountains. Remember how we…"

Chapter Twenty

Susannah reached the house and talked to the girls about the cake. She didn't say anything about Joshua, Jane knew it wasn't her place to ask, and Lydia had grown too shy to even glance out the windows. So she kept the young ladies busy into the afternoon. There was bathing and hemming, stitching and reading, then time to start supper and the cake.

"It smells incredible," Lucas called out as he stepped inside of the house. He always said that but the girls still beamed and Susannah felt a smile on her lips. That smile of his made her heart thump harder as he looked her way.

"What?" she asked, hands deep in the mixing bowl when his gaze didn't leave. She blushed, knowing she was covered in flour and her hair was half out of its braid. If anything, the man was about to start laughing.

The two girls didn't notice as they hummed, distracted with their work. Susannah raised her eyebrow and was determined not to let his stare affect her when he finally spoke up quietly, "You really are beautiful, even now."

"Even now?" she echoed, and raised an eyebrow. "Is it not enough flour to charm you? Should I put a little more on my nose? Why, I even washed my feet for you." She showed off her bare foot. "Isn't that enough?"

He headed to their room to wash up, laughing. It made her grin and she turned back, finishing the icing for the cake that would be cooling down soon. Susannah glanced over at it by the sink, and saw Lydia walk by again, bending over to inhale the sweet spice scent. Holding back a laugh, she shook her head and kept stirring.

When Lucas returned, he was dressed in a clean shirt, had combed his hair, and even brought out the fiddle. Her heart surged with excitement and instantly Susannah felt like a young girl again, attending her first dance. Putting down the finished cake, Susannah cheered louder than the other girls.

"Do play something for us, dear." She hurried over and watched him check each string carefully before placing the instrument beneath his chin.

They sang together—a song they knew well. She clapped and started to dance a few steps, the girls following along. With Lucas busy playing the fiddle, Susannah took Lydia in her arms first, and danced them around the room. That was one of the many lessons she and Lucas taught them, and it was one of her favorites. The way one could express their joy like that, it made her heart smile.

Lydia laughed and made way for Jane to take her turn. Susannah spun the girl around the chairs, away from all the food. This was Jane's hardest lesson, for the clumsiness always grew worse the more she had to move. But with a steady rhythm and Susannah's sure touch, the young lady managed to stay on her toes, and off anyone else's.

"Now you two," she instructed cheerfully, bringing Lydia back into the mix. Lucas paused from singing to cheer them on, and turned it into another lively tune. Susannah knew the words better than he did, and took up the singing. Just as she glanced towards the window, she saw a figure stepping up on the porch, and hurried to the door.

Quietly Joshua stepped through and she put a hand close to her lips as she sang, seeing how the two young ladies were still twirling and laughing. They crossed the room and back without even noticing their company. Susannah watched him for a second, and suddenly knew.

There were the little things, things she had noticed all her life but never realized that she knew for a long time. Like the way Joshua immediately straightened, and a brightness shone in his eyes.

Jane was taller with dark hair, and Lydia was slighter with long, blond hair. It flew loose, framing her face beautifully. And Joshua saw the girl she had told him about. Not just her appearance, but the joy. He pulled off his hat and she caught it before it fell to the ground, the man too distracted to notice.

She caught her breath and murmured, "It's your turn. Girls, switch!" And they did it automatically, the way she had taught them. It was sheer luck, Susannah realized, that Joshua knew what to do. Susannah's hands wrapped around Jane's and the two pairs were down the hall before anyone realized another man had entered the house, let alone the dance. She heard it in Lydia's gasp. That's when Jane faltered, and her shoulder brushed against the wall.

It wasn't enough to catch anyone's notice but Susannah's, and she stopped singing and dancing in the next breath. Jane apologized sheepishly, rubbing her shoulder as they turned to watch Joshua whisk Lydia back towards the front door where Lucas brought the song to an end.

The idea had been sudden and there was no guarantee it would work. But Lydia needed to grow up and be reminded that she hadn't come here to play. No, it was to start a new life. A grown-up life with this man.

Susannah watched carefully, walking over to stand beside her husband who gave her an appraising look. It wasn't like her to rush an introduction after all, not when everything hinged on this moment.

Lucas put a hand on Susannah's shoulder as Lydia's hands slipped out of Joshua's and the young girl looked away shyly. The man was over a head taller than her, and older. He was more experienced, and made wise by his trials.

Joshua stepped to the side of Lydia and unconsciously, Lydia pushed her hair out of her eyes. Susannah heard Jane pull in a deep breath. With the hair away from Lydia's face, he would see the scars. Of course, Joshua knew about them, but Susannah had never focused Lydia's scars in her correspondence with him. Lydia was so much more than her past and her scars.

She had no idea she was holding her own breath until Joshua cleared his throat. "My apologies, madam, for interrupting the dance. I know I must have caught you by surprise, but... I didn't want to wait any longer. I wanted to join the fun and dance with you. I can leave if you like. I hardly expect you were prepared, and I would hate to interrupt any more merriment."

It took Lydia a long moment to catch her breath.

Joshua glanced hesitantly up at the married couple, who nodded for him to hold his place. Just last week at church, Lydia had been spoken to by another young man, one who was only asking to step around her to meet his girl when Lydia had frozen up. She was used to Lucas, perhaps because of Susannah, but it was clearly something that needed to be worked through. And who best than her own husband to be? Although, Susannah decided, the silence had gone on long enough. She was just about to pipe up impatiently when Lydia nodded.

"Stay," she whispered and then cleared her throat. "Please. I'd like you to stay. I'm sure you might even add to our merriment. My name is Lydia Cowell and I came here from New York."

A small smile slipped onto Joshua's tired face. Even from a few yards Susannah could see the crinkling of the man's eyes. "It's a pleasure to meet you, Miss Lydia. I'm Joshua Ralph, and I came by way of Nevada."

"Did you bring the horses, then?"

He nodded. "Over a hundred."

"A hundred!" Lydia clasped her hands together. "Oh, you must tell me. Were they wild? Beautiful?" And all the shyness had dissipated. Susannah beamed and turned to Lucas who nodded. She had been right.

"Jane, shall we bring out supper?" Susannah turned to the other girl, and led her to the kitchen. Lucas followed, trailing and singing that song of theirs on the fiddle. Jane brought out the bread and fruit basket as she grabbed the lemonade, leaving the cake on the counter.

Susannah looked at the girl and smiled her most encouraging smile. "Jane, tonight you're hosting. Invite the other guests in and have them seated."

Chapter Twenty-One

Rocky Ridge, Colorado; 1876

It had been three months, one week, and four days since she had told him what she knew to be true. It had been one month, two weeks, and one day since she'd fallen by the barn and grown ill. And it had been almost a month since she felt well enough to go about her chores again.

Their routine had been good for the last few years, but it had been altered after she had revealed her belief that she was barren. That day burned in her memory, and she kept turning back to it. Susannah couldn't stay busy enough to forget, and it dragged her down. And as they started a new routine, she wasn't sure she liked it much better.

He returned to sleeping in their bed, though he tried to keep space between them. Even though he kept to early mornings, she was always asleep when he arose, though she was up half the night. Lucas was there for every meal, ensuring she ate at least half her plate, and then he would leave. There was polite conversation, nightly reading, but little else said.

After a month, Susannah decided to bring it up again.

She had been patient with his struggles as he had been patient with her need for healing. But she reasoned with herself that since it was something that they had to endure together, they had to come to terms and truly accept this. He'd said he wouldn't leave her, so the barrier he had put between them had to be eradicated.

But how?

Susannah studied him from the porch, a shawl wrapped tightly around her shoulders. Though it was summer, she still shivered. Her clothes still felt loose on her, though she knew she had gained some of the weight back. Slowly her appetite was returning, and they were making things work. They hadn't taken any boarders in months, a rarity, but she decided it was probably a smart move.

"Here." She brought him a glass of water as he worked, fixing her horse's harness. Star noticed her and neighed softly, since they hadn't seen each other in a while.

Lucas glanced at her in surprise. "Thank you." He accepted it and drank as she stepped over to her horse's stall. Once he had drained it, he set it on the workshop table and continued working with the leather. "She misses you, you know."

Biting the inside of her cheek, she nodded. "I've missed her, too." After a minute, she gathered the courage to ask him, "Why don't we take a ride tomorrow, into the mountains? It's been a while. We could go after church."

She saw his shoulders tense, and it made her heart drop. He didn't look at her then, but stared extra hard at his project. "I don't know about that. You're still gathering your strength, Susannah. It might be too much for you."

"But I feel well," she protested, still clinging to her

shawl as Star nudged her shoulder. "Enough for a ride and I won't be walking. The fresh air would do me well, if anything. And you would be there if anything happened."

Sighing, he turned and their gazes met. The man looked at her in resignation, and she knew he had to be as tired of this as she was. So why couldn't they just fix this? Why was he so difficult?

"Your harness isn't ready." He picked it up and showed her. "It'll need a few days before it's usable again."

The man was about to turn away but she skipped over to him. "Then I'll ride with you," she offered. "Your horse can carry us both, he's done it before. And we'll keep it short, stick to the trail. Please?" She asked for little enough, and Susannah sought his gaze hopefully.

She saw him swallow and then his eyes came up to meet hers. Dark brown and expressive, they flickered with an expression she wasn't sure she understood or even liked. Was it pain? Disdain for her? It worried her, making her wonder if she would lose him for good, even if he stayed. The idea that they would be in this strange routine for the rest of their lives scared her.

"A short one," he said finally, and her heart skipped a beat in relief. "After we've eaten and you've rested."

"I accept your terms." She nodded and couldn't suppress a smile. Susannah considered leaving then, but felt drawn to him, not wanting to leave his side. Though he didn't appear to want her there with him, the young woman turned to her horse and pulled out a brush. Star needed some attention, she decided, and that way she would still be around him as they both tended to what needed to be done.

Chapter Twenty-Two

Once his terms were met Sunday afternoon, she went to him where he was taking care of the apple trees. Straightening her jacket, Susannah beamed. "I'm ready for our ride, Lucas."

Turning to her, Lucas frowned and looked her over. Her smile faded as he spoke, "I thought you needed more rest. You look pale. Peaked."

She had sat in the sun room for two hours, shuffling through the Bible, unable to truly focus on what she was reading.

Weighing her options, she shook her head. "No, I'll be fine. I am fine. If I start to feel faint, I'll tell you. Besides, you said it would be a short ride and with you, I'm not likely to fall. It would be nice to spend some time with you."

"We do spend time together," he muttered, turning away from inspecting the trees. "Every day."

She frowned. "I suppose we do. But not the way we used to. I miss that. You never talk to me, and it's…well, it's just not like it was before. I miss it." As Lucas headed off towards the house, she trailed after him. Though she knew she should probably wait for him to speak, she couldn't stop talking. "We don't have conversations like we used to and we certainly never touch. I feel like you only look at me to make sure I'm eating, which makes me feel like a child with you as my caretaker."

He stopped at the table, and Susannah realized that might have been a poor choice of words. Seeing the stiffness in his shoulders, it made her want to cry for messing up all over again.

Though he turned to face her, he didn't say anything. And for a minute, neither could she. Her heart jumped and grew stuck in her throat and she felt the tears swimming at the brim, ready to escape down her cheeks. Even as she tried to calmly raise a hand to hurriedly wipe one away, Susannah hiccupped and they started falling in a rainstorm. Within moments, she was bawling.

"Don't touch me," she cried when he reached out for her. Susannah turned red, ashamed and embarrassed and angry.

Sighing, Lucas shook his head. "Sit down, please. You're tired. You should let me take you to bed for a nap—"

He pulled out a chair for her and she swiped his hand away. "No, Lucas. You can't keep doing this. You can't act like nothing is wrong. Because something is wrong, and it's all my fault. You can't say you care and then treat me like...you can't treat me like this."

As her hands scrubbed at her face frantically in the hopes of seeing clearly again, she felt his hands wrap around her shoulders to calm her. Sniffling, she watched his blurry form kneel before her. "I told you—"

"You've had months!" She pushed him away again, trying to catch her breath. "I know this is hard, but it's hard for me, too. You're not the only one who's devastated. Don't you see it? You're letting this tear us apart when we should be leaning on each other."

Lucas stared at her for a minute as she hiccupped again, and tried to find her handkerchief. After she had rubbed her eyes and blown her nose, her husband slowly brought forth his own which she used in the same manner. Though she worked on her breathing, it occasionally caught and she wiped away any more tears with her jacket sleeve. For several minutes the two of them remained still, gathering their emotions.

Finally, she shook her head. "It's probably never going to be easy. My aunt told me about how it's been for her. She sometimes wakes up in a sweat after she's dreamed of a child. It may not get better, don't you get it? I won't suddenly feel better about not having children. It's a scar that doesn't go away, and your polite silence will remind me of my failing every day of my life."

He looked down at the floor and remained silent.

"Lucas, you have an option. You could have children if you truly wanted. But I never will."

"I told you I keep my promises."

Their eyes met. "And I've given you leave to break it." She swallowed hard, but didn't look away. "If you choose to stay, I want all of you. I don't want to live with a man who seems to despise me. So, if you choose to stay married to me, you'll need to keep all of the promise we made to each other on our wedding day. The for better or for worse part. Does that mean anything to you?" Her speech came off more harshly than she had expected or intended, and she could see the hurt in his eyes. Still, she didn't back down.

Lucas finally stretched forth his hands and took hers

in his. She could feel their rough warmth as they buried hers away between his long fingers. He wore a pained, raw expression as he took a deep breath. "For better or for worse. That means to take what happens, come what may," he sighed and closed his eyes. "You're a brash woman, Susannah Tumlin Jessup, but I love you for it."

She glanced at their hands uncertainly, unsure of what he was trying to say. Biting the inside of her cheek, the young woman sniffled and tried to read his eyes.

"I miss you," she managed meekly. "Your smiles, your comments about the food, your jokes. I want my husband back."

He stood up, and brought her up with him. The handkerchiefs went on the table, and Lucas Jessup took his beloved wife in his arms. Susannah drew in a deep breath, inhaling his rough scent of cedar, leather, and manly sweat. Slowly wrapping her arms around his neck, she felt the unruliness of his hair as he cradled her with his arms tightly wound around her.

"I'm here, Susie darling. I'm here."

And for a minute, they stood there, taking deep breaths and settling their nerves. It was exhausting, the crying and confessing of her soul. He kept her on her feet and they swayed lightly. Susannah wiped away the last tear, one of gratitude that Lucas was still there. He had looked her in the eye, and now she knew that things could be better. Things would most definitely be better.

Finally, he sighed, and loosened his grip only just. "Let's get you to bed, shall we?"

She was about to agree, but stopped. "No. Our ride, please?" Susannah looked at him hopefully, though she knew she was a mess. Her face would be red and puffy, but if she went to rest now, then Lucas would leave her there alone until the evening. And she wasn't ready for that yet.

"You don't even like being on my horse," he reminded her. "You think his gait is awkward."

"For starters," she sniffed, "it is. But it's less annoying with you," she added. "And just a short ride. We don't even need to leave the yard. I like our Sunday rides. Don't you?"

He sighed. "Yes, I do. Then let's go, before you fall asleep on me."

That made her shoot him a look. "I wouldn't do that."

"Oh wouldn't you?" But he was starting to smile now, and it lifted her heart. A weight slipped off her shoulders that Susannah hadn't realized had been weighing her down. As Lucas led her out to the barn, she wondered what would happen now.

They could take in more boarders, she decided as he helped her onto the stallion. And after all of her preparations for having a family, that would go away and give her the time to do something else. Perhaps she could start her own business, Susannah marveled, and reminded herself that Eleanor was on her way. When the young woman arrived, she made a note to talk to the girl about how to best spend her energies from then on.

She sat near the pommel with Lucas's arms wrapped around her. "Are you ready?"

He gathered the reins and they started to move.

It didn't matter what tomorrow would bring so long as she had him by her side. And besides, they could find other things to keep themselves busy. Tomorrow would be a good day. Surely, she thought to herself, a better day, and a better one after that.

Chapter Twenty-Three

Rocky Ridge, Colorado; 1882

The evening with Joshua Ralph went well, though Lydia's shyness returned occasionally. But she accepted a stroll with her intended beneath the trees after cake, where they talked for nearly an hour. He had brought his bedrolls and took to the loft in their barn once the evening came to an end.

Since Joshua had the time to spare, he stayed for another week, often trailing Lucas around. This gave Susannah the rest of the time she needed and time Lydia wanted, to ensure she was ready to head off to Nevada for her new life.

She and Jane helped Lydia prepare for her wedding, a lovely little affair with their nearest neighbor there and the pastor to officiate. It was performed beneath the apple trees, at Lydia's request. Afterwards, she threw her small bouquet of wildflowers to Jane, laughing and blushing.

And then, the young girl was on her way to Nevada. "I'll write to you, all of you. I promise!" She waved madly as Joshua slipped an arm around her waist to keep her from bouncing off the wagon. After blowing Susannah a kiss, the young bride turned back to her husband and they were gone.

It was only early morning then, and they were hoping to make good time by nightfall. With the sun just up on the horizon, Susannah sighed and melted into Lucas's arms behind her. "They're going to be happy," she whispered softly to him. "I just know it."

A chuckle rumbled through his throat. "Of course, they are. You're always right, darling."

She grinned. "I know. But I mean it. I can see it in them, Lucas. They're going to be so good for each other. Did you see the way they looked at one another? It's like…" she searched for words and turned to him. "It's like they've woken up and realized what the next day will bring them. And the next, and the next."

The man raised an eyebrow. "That sounds very boring."

She hit his shoulder lightly. "Not in every moment, but that every moment will have a purpose. We find this in the Lord, but in life we have that when…when we have the one He chose for us."

Jane had already gone inside, tying an apron around her waist to start making bread for the rest of the week. They were alone with the rising sun at the edge of their yard. Lucas's arms were loosely draped around her waist, and his soft gaze made her want to melt.

"You mean like this?" He kissed her cheek, but barely. "Or this?" He kissed the other, and it felt more like a whisper against her skin. "Or this?" That third time, his lips brushed her own, and she smiled.

Pressing their foreheads together, she nodded slowly.

"Exactly like that." She kissed him again and then opened her eyes. "Now, I just realized that Jane may not know how much bread to make."

He gave her a pretend exasperated expression, overly exaggerated to make her giggle. "We were having a nice moment."

"That could end with the house on fire or Jane burning herself or some other terrible thing," she reminded him, and tugged him towards the house. "Come on. Let's go." The man grumbled under his breath as she pulled them back to the house.

Chapter Twenty-Four

"Am I ever going to leave?" Jane mumbled the afternoon after Lydia left with her new husband. It was just her then, and now there was more free time that they didn't know what to do with. The girl leaned against the porch railing and sighed, fiddling with her apron. But then realizing that Susannah had heard, she gasped and turned bright red. "Oh! Mrs. Jessup! I didn't mean, um, I don't mean like—"

But she didn't mind. Looping her arm through hers, she guided Jane inside. "That's all right dear. And yes, you will. In about two weeks."

A nice man had written to her soon after Rosie had left. She had prayed about it and talked it over with Lucas. Two letters later, it was decided. Jane now had those letters that Susannah knew she looked at often, and the young girl was anxious to meet the man she would marry.

"Two weeks?" Jane started. "That soon? I didn't know it was set."

It made her laugh. "You were just worrying about being here too long! And yes, I was going to tell you tonight. I got final word yesterday."

The young woman stumbled over her words, brushing her hair from her face and apprehensively trying to decide what she felt. "Well, I, um, I mean I only…what if I don't—or if he doesn't like me? Or I…oh, Mrs. Jessup!" She leapt forward and hugged Susannah warmly. "I can hardly believe it!"

Laughing, Susannah squeezed her in return and wondered how the girl would manage over the next two weeks. "Well you had better believe it. And we still need to get you ready. There are a few dresses to hem and your sewing needs to improve."

Stepping back, Jane gave her a rueful smile and held up her hand that carried two new bandages on the tips of her fingers. "Don't I know it," she said and took a deep breath, eyes bright and filled with hope. "Let's begin!"

And the young woman, now focused on a goal with an end date, drove herself forward. She became brighter and more energetic than Lydia had ever been. It made Susannah think, wondering what was on her mind, and if it was the same that hers had been back in the beginning.

Chapter Twenty-Five

Rocky Ridge, Colorado; 1873

Winter had melted into spring and a sweltering summer, and they'd had their first Christmas together. She had given him a new shirt, and he'd found her some flower pots to start growing wildflowers in the window. Together, they had made taffy and he'd pulled out his fiddle for the first time.

"I didn't know you could play an instrument," she had mused, delighted to find something new in the house. Where could it have been hiding? Susannah had been certain she had scrubbed and cleaned every inch of the house, except, of course, she realized, his wardrobe in their bedroom. She didn't want to intrude, and he never asked that she clean it. Thus, it could contain just about anything and she would never know.

He gave her a sheepish smile. "I don't, not really. Not for years. But it's an occasion, isn't it?"

She nodded and smiled brightly overcome with happiness at finding out something new about her husband.

After tweaking the strings, he slipped the instrument

beneath his chin and tested them. They squeaked painfully and she tried not to wince. "Sorry." He cleared his throat and after two tries, he managed to find the right note.

Inhaling deeply, Susannah nodded and clasped her hands beneath her chin to listen. After a few lines, the man attempted to sing as well, a silly grin slipping onto his face. "'Adown by the murmuring stream, that merrily winds through the valley, I wandered in days that are gone. With the joy of my heart'—Susie." He changed the name at the last second which caught her by surprise.

"Don't be ridiculous," she interrupted his song with a laugh, though she urged him to go on with a wave of her hands. "Use the right names, Lucas."

He finished the song as he wanted it to be without listening to her protests. At the end, he paused and turned to her. "I can fit your name in any song I like, you know."

There was a small gleam in his eye and her mouth dropped open, surprised at him. Lucas had a side of humor and childishness that he didn't show often, and it always caught her off guard. "No, you can't. I am sure my name is in a song or two, but—"

He interrupted her with the fiddle and a new song. "Oh, my Susie. Oh, my Susie. Oh, my darling Susannah. Now you are gone and lost forever, I'm dreadful sorry, Susannah."

Well, he was just being ridiculous. But she still laughed. The man wore a cheeky smile as he drew closer and tapped his boots. The melody changed and she gave in, clapping her hands and singing along with him.

"Well I come from Alabama with my banjo on my

knee, and I'm bound for Louisiana, my own true love for to see. It did rain all night the day I left, the weather was bone dry. The sun was so hot I froze to death, Susannah, don't you cry. I said oh, Susannah, now, don't you cry for me, as I come from Alabama with this banjo on my knee!"

He whooped and the song ended with a flourish as she clapped louder.

"M'lady." He set down the instrument and gave her a low bow with remarkable ease.

Restraining a giggle, she picked up her skirts to curtsey, and then took his hand. Immediately the man pulled her close and she inhaled sharply. The now familiar tingle ran up and down her spine as she entwined her fingers with his and her other hand gripped his shoulder.

After one look, Lucas's grave expression disappeared with a wink and he led her around the house in a dance. He hummed in her ear, keeping in perfect tune and deftly making their way around the furniture. They fit together like a hand in a glove and he never let her bump into a wall or table.

"Whoa," she breathed softly as they came to an end, but there was hardly a grand flourish. Her heart beat loudly inside her chest, and Susannah wondered if he could hear. But even his chest rose and caved deeply, and she smiled.

The man's eyes met hers and she lost herself in their depth. Right now they held more warmth than any hearth she'd ever warmed her hands over.

"You dance beautifully," he murmured softly.

She smiled. "Only because you lead me so well."

"And I'd do it a thousand times more."

"I'd love that," Susannah felt the words slip off her

tongue more lightly than the way he held her. "I love you."

She didn't even register the words until she noticed a flicker of movement in his brow. It moved with serious thought, and she immediately sucked in air, eyes widening. The words had slipped out and she hadn't thought to catch them.

Neither of them had said those words before, to each other or anyone else. Suddenly her heart moved up into her throat, and she felt lightheaded but mostly foolish for letting her feelings escape. Susannah searched for something else to say, desperately wishing to salvage her dignity and pride. She was worried that the whole day would be ruined because of a lapse in control.

Just as she thought he was loosening his grip and about to step away, Lucas drew her even closer with their bodies pressed together as he leaned down to kiss her. There had been few kisses between them like this one. Usually they were gentle, a little shy. Some were firm, as if he wanted to show his appreciation for her. And then there had been those special occasions where it felt like they couldn't get enough of one another.

Somehow, this one was different from all the others.

Lucas was delicate as he touched her, as though he were worried he would bruise her. The moment took her breath away and she didn't want to let go. Her hands found his arms, making sure he didn't leave her. She felt his hand lightly graze her arm until he finally caressed her cheek. They were warm and big, and made Susannah feel as though he was double her size. She felt small and feminine and it was a wonderful feeling.

When Lucas began to pull away, hesitatingly as though he were worried she didn't want his touch, Susannah immediately made the space between them dissipate as she met his lips, pulling him back in just as he had done for her.

And just like that, she couldn't help the words slipping back out between kisses. "I do," she whispered, and he kissed the corners of her lips teasingly. "I can't help it. I don't want to help it. I just wanted you to know." He reached over to touch her chin. "I do love you."

He halted, and Susannah worried she had continued to misread the situation somehow. But then he looked at her gravely, an expression he rarely deemed worthy of an occasion. "And I love you, too."

She didn't have time to sigh in relief before he gave her one more, long and rather sweet kiss.

Chapter Twenty-Six

Rocky Ridge, Colorado; 1882

My goodness, that had been a good kiss, Susannah thought to herself, and giggled lightly. There had been many more kisses along the way, of course, and it seemed as though he always had one ready for her.

"What are you thinking about, Mrs. Jessup?" Jane interrupted her day dreams, peering at her curiously. Together they were sitting near the fire, and Susannah looked down at her lap to find a pair of Lucas's pants that he'd ripped just the other day.

Susannah opened her mouth to reply, but recalled just in time that she needed to think of a better answer. That is, a more acceptable and modest answer. "Lucas and his love of the pigs," she said at last. "He named them, you know."

The young girl nodded with a little grin. "So I heard. Sampson, John, and what was the other one?"

"I don't know," Susannah lied and shook her head. "But tomorrow its name is Supper, and I'm rather uncertain if he'll be able to get the task done."

Jane made a face. Back in Boston, she could go down to the butcher shop for anything they needed. But here, you had to be your own butcher. She didn't mind the chickens, plucking the feathers and the like. But she had been reluctant to take the pigs on when he'd decided he wanted them for Christmas, and her feelings hadn't changed since.

Jane inhaled deeply, and fell quiet. She didn't even laugh so Susannah looked up and immediately realized that the young girl's mind was already far away, most likely thinking of Robert Malcomb.

He was a cousin of William Malcomb from Colorado Springs, and was moving to Denver. Susannah had matched William up with a lovely young lady from Virginia, and he had referred his cousin to her. After Robert's letters, she'd decided that he and Jane would be a good fit.

And tomorrow was the day. They'd seen each other twice in passing but hadn't had the opportunity to speak yet. So close, and yet so far. Susannah knew it was time to remedy that so she set up a grand supper for the two to meet. They were even making pie again. She was hoping it would result in a wedding by Saturday, next.

"Jane?" Susannah asked softly. "Are you all right?"

The girl bit her lip and nodded. "Yes, I think I am. I truly am happy, you know," she added hurriedly. "And excited. He looked kind, and I only hope I'm not too clumsy to send him running away."

Shaking her head, Susannah reminded her, "That's not the important thing. Remember that. Give him a chance to get to know you, and take the opportunity to get to know him. And of course, you're making that pie all on your own."

Jane looked up nervously but then shook her head with a little smile. Worries never kept this girl down for longer than a second lately. "That sounds wonderful." She cleared her throat. "I'll pick the berries first thing in the morning."

It made Susannah proud to see the young girl growing in all of her accomplishments. It wasn't so much that she raised them to be wives, she believed, but to be strong and talented women. If anything happened to their husbands, then they were more than ready to take charge and could run any household immediately.

Lucas taught them the basics of hunting rabbits, riding, and some shooting as well, to make sure they could survive if necessary. Though a beautiful land, it was only for the strong. And she made sure that these women were the strongest of them all.

When they were finishing up their needle projects, Susannah heard horses trotting into the yard. With a short glance out the window, she saw Lucas climb down, back for the evening. He stood straight, she noticed when she looked again, and uninjured. Since their marriage, she couldn't help but appraise the man on his return home to make sure he'd made it in one piece. The only thing that stood out now was that he had two horses now instead of one.

"Why don't you see to the fire?" Susannah stood up and put the patched clothes in the basket. "Let's get some potatoes on to roast and slice some cheese. I'll join you in a minute." Before stepping outside, she grabbed a bucket as an excuse and headed out.

Susannah held the bucket close to her ribs as she wondered about the new animal. Lucas had disappeared into the barn with his stallion, but this was a smaller

horse, chestnut red, loosely tied right outside the barn-
yard doors.

In Boston, they'd had plenty of horses to ride and to
drive the carriages. But they were expensive and there
was never an occasion that had required Susannah to
ride. For this reason, she had never sat upon a horse
until that first spring when Lucas had discovered that
she didn't know how to ride.

The big animals were pretty, but they weren't always nice in the city. In fact, they could be downright
dangerous and no matter how gorgeous they were, the
creatures scared Susannah. Lucas had two horses in the
beginning. His young stallion and a pack horse for the
wagon and farming had been all he really needed. He
liked to take care of them, so she had never even fed
them. Until he learned about her fear and insisted that
she change her ways.

With time, Susannah had come to love the mare he
had bought her. The horse was white and brown and
not very big. She had been named Star, and loved big
red apples and the thickest carrots. And more impor-
tantly, Susannah loved riding her, since her walking
style didn't jostle her around. Lucas's own stallion had
such a stiff step, she didn't know how Lucas managed.

"Isn't she beautiful?"

She dropped her bucket as she jumped, not having
noticed her husband there. Giving her an apologetic
smile, the man picked up the fallen pail and glanced in
her empty container. "Looks like you still have some
work ahead of you. Or, mayhap, you were wondering
about this most perfect beauty?"

Susannah tried to smile. "I thought I was the most
beautiful one."

"You are." He nodded, and draped an arm around her shoulders. "Which is why I found the most beautiful horse that I could possibly manage. And before you protest," Lucas started when she opened her mouth, "this little filly came from Joshua's stock and was a gift for you. I wanted to wait until things settled down, and I've been doing some training with her in the stables in town."

Biting her lip, Susannah allowed him to put the bucket down by their feet, and he started guiding her around to see the front of the animal. She had to be just a little smaller than Star, she decided, and looked softer. Why, even after the ride here from the center of Rocky Ridge, the horse's mane barely looked touched. "She's very soft," she whispered as she lightly stroked her neck.

He nodded. "Hardly a year old, and very gentle. Josh had been keeping an eye on her since the day she was born. He said the other horses frightened her, so he gave her some special treatment, and the sweet girl perked right on up. But he knew she wouldn't be appropriate for long hauls or any hard riding, and we knew she could be just perfect for you."

For a minute she considered it. It was much too gracious a gift, Susannah knew, even from a good friend. But with Joshua gone, she couldn't turn down the offer and that's probably why Lucas hadn't said anything.

"Well?"

"Don't rush me," she said immediately, and he gave her a look. "Sorry," she amended, and squeezed his hand. "What if she doesn't like me? What if she doesn't have a smooth gait? I don't want to hurt her, or turn her down. Or get hurt," she added after a heartbeat.

Lucas just shook his head. "You're thinking about this too much. Horses are smart, remember? I promise you, this little filly has the energy to do whatever she pleases, but likes to be a lady more than anything. You give her some special treatment, and she'll ride smoother than if you two could walk on water." She raised her eyebrow at the analogy but the man just shrugged, and began to tug her forward. "Before you get all panicked, at least give her a try."

So, she did. Reaching up to the rope harness, Susannah took a deep breath and stepped close enough to touch the young horse again. The animal looked at her curiously through thick lashes, nodding as though she understood how nervous Susannah was. The creature nickered quietly as Susannah breathed softly into her nostrils, and carefully brushed her fingers along the nose.

Within moments, it was apparent to them both that they would be friends. "I told you so," Lucas murmured, coming up from behind to rest his chin on the top of her head as Susannah ran her fingers through the gorgeous mane. "What are you going to name her?"

His breath tickled her cheek and she smiled. "Sunny."

Lucas chuckled. "You and your pet names. I like it."

"Better than Sampson," she reminded him.

The man objected, "He's in the Bible. You can't get better than that."

"For a pig? You know he's food, don't you?"

"Of course, I do. But everyone deserves a name and, you know, it seemed good at the time..." Lucas trailed off and grinned. "I don't know. I feel like it kind of fits him. If he really wanted, Sampson the pig could break those fences and run to freedom."

Laughing, Susannah shook her head as she took the rope harness that led her new horse, and started into the barn. "You'd better hope that doesn't happen. After all, it would be your responsibility to rebuild whatever he breaks."

He just winked, and she focused on brushing down the horse. As she quickly discovered, the young filly preened and loved every minute of care, shaking her head back and forth and whistling through her nose softly. Whenever Susannah stood close enough to her head, Sunny would lean forward and nudge her gently, as though to let her know she was doing a good job— and that she shouldn't stop. Susannah was still chuckling as she left and returned towards the house.

There, Lucas was filling up her bucket with vegetables from the garden. Grinning, she placed the last cucumber on top. "Why thank you." She nodded graciously as he picked it up for her. "And I do mean it," the woman added after a moment, touching his arm. "I'm excited to ride her."

"Good." His brow cleared. "That will be good. Perhaps we can return to our Sunday rides. You haven't seen the flowers up on our hill."

She opened the door for him. "You're right, I haven't. And it's about time."

Chapter Twenty-Seven

After giving her husband a kiss on the cheek, Susannah pulled the door closed behind them and helped him pull his jacket off. As her husband left to wash up, she headed to the kitchen to see how Jane was coming along with supper.

They were putting together the last of the meal when Lucas returned and brought out some papers from his jacket. He traded those for the plates Susannah pulled out, and she glanced through them. One was a letter from Lydia, a quickly scribbled greeting filled with gratitude and joy, with a promise for a longer letter soon.

One was from her aunt Sally, still checking in with her after all this time. Over the last couple of years, Ruby had passed away, and Mary only wrote during the holidays. It was sad, but she knew there were other things more important. Even her parents wrote rarely since there was nothing new to share because nothing changed in Boston for them.

And the third was a letter from Rhode Island. Curious, Susannah stepped towards a candle as she opened it up, finding a pretty little scribble. The unfamiliar script made sense, however, and Susannah knew without reading a single word that it was about a new girl inquiring about a potential match to a man from the western territories.

To Mrs. Susannah Jessup of the Mountainside Residence for Women,

I send you greetings from Rhode Island, where it is windy but gray and green. I have enjoyed living here all of my life. However, I address you now in the hopes of leaving this place and never returning. Word of you and your services has reached my parts and though most of it is based on rumors, I wanted to seek you out in the hopes of influencing my own future.

As I'm sure you can tell from my writing, I have been raised well and am well educated. My family comes from a bit of money and while they believe themselves to be ready for the turn of the century, they forget I am a woman with my own voice. For all intents and purposes, I come with a rather large dowry on top of everything else and for that reason, I know I have low expectations and little hope of finding a good man here. I'm sure there are decent ones, but none that will be considered or esteemed highly enough to win my family's favor, and I couldn't even begin to trust anyone when all they must see is money.

I am only seventeen years old, but I come into my inheritance next year and the dowry by my twenty-first birthday. It is only by heading out west, to a place where no one will know of my name or money, that I believe I can find a marriage based on the better principles of the Lord's way, and if I'm so fortunate, joy.

From what I understand, you help women find a man to settle down with. And you do it with the help of the Lord. Please write back to me if I have misunderstood, and I will endeavor to change my understanding. And if I am correct, please write me back all the same and let me find a way out of this dreary life I now lead. My parents are plotting an engagement even as I speak, and I have had to sneak this letter from the house since I have mentioned you before and they did not approve. I will not have my parents' blessing as a mail order bride, I am afraid, but I believe I have the Lord's.

I will watch for your letter with high hopes,
Miss Emmaline Mary-Elizabeth Buchanan

Susannah read it through a second time, her eyebrows arched more highly during the second reading. It was different than the other letters she usually received. Most of the girls that came to her had problems that kept them from being a desirable wife. Some had disfigurements or were less attractive than other girls of marriageable age in their towns. All of them needed help finding a husband.

This girl was rather young, and definitely refined. It was not what Susannah had in mind when she had started her Mountainside Residence. She had a heart for helping those who needed it the most.

But didn't she give all girls a chance? Folding it up, she decided to speak to her husband about this one.

Shaking her head, she put the letter in her pocket and took a seat as Jane and Lucas brought over the last items for their supper.

"Is everything all right?" Jane asked her politely, pausing before filling her glass with lemonade.

She smiled tentatively. "Everything is fine, but thank you for asking. Now, would you mind saying grace tonight?" The girl nodded and clasped her hands as Susannah felt her husband's gaze on her. He rose an eyebrow questioningly, and she nodded to confirm what had gone unsaid. Another letter, another girl.

It wasn't until after supper was finished, cleaned up, and they were settling in their rooms for the evening when Susannah brought it up. She slipped the note from her dress pocket for him to read. She curled up on their bed, brushing her long hair as he studiously read the letter.

Lucas is such a handsome man and I'm so grateful for his kind nature. Susannah's thoughts wandered as she watched him. Even with the scar, he always had been the most handsome man in the world to her. Granted, now she hardly even noticed it.

He was a quiet type of beautiful. Rugged and re-strained. Over the last many years, Susannah had cherished every moment in learning about the man. He still surprised her with his talents, his words, and that sense of humor. Biting her lip, she paused and couldn't wait any longer. "Well?"

As he set the letter down, her husband frowned. "While her parents are still her legal guardians, anything that happens, even if it's her decision, would bode ill for us. We could even be arrested for kidnapping."

"Even if you're the sheriff?" She tried to joke, but

he was serious as he took off his shirt and joined her on the bed. Sighing, Susannah fiddled with her hair brush and eyed his chest. No bruises at the moment. He was solid and strong, but his chest and back was covered in even more scars. "You know I hate to say no, Lucas. Is there anything we could do? At all?"

Picking up the brush, Lucas leaned against the headboard and began combing her hair for her. The longer his strokes grew, the more she felt the tension ebbing out of her. It was a solid two minutes before he said anything.

"I don't blame the young lady for wanting an escape, but we can't do anything while her parents are her guardians. While you know I don't like tearing a family apart, as long as she isn't married or under age by the time she gets here, then she can do anything she likes. But I'm concerned that perhaps they may come after her, or she may lose her money. It doesn't sound like she's taken that into consideration."

Closing her eyes, Susannah sighed and tried to think. She felt the brush weaving through her thick hair, starting at the top of her head and trailing all the way down her back. Whenever Lucas came upon a knot, he gently wove his fingers through the strands to keep the work pain free for her.

With an absent smile, she sighed again and knew he was right. "I'll tell her that," she said decidedly. "We can keep writing, and I'll even look through the possible bachelors. And if this is something she really, truly wants, then we'll help her."

Their gazes met. "After she's eighteen."

Neither of them liked it, but she accepted this. "After she's eighteen," she repeated, and smiled at him.

"You're such a smart man." Kissing his cheek, she took the brush and put it down to put her hair in a braid.

"Good night, my love," he murmured as he blew out the lantern.

As she settled down beneath the covers, Lucas found her hand and kissed it lightly. She turned to him, smiling in the moonlight. "Good night, Lucas." And for once, she managed to make it through the entire night sleeping without waking up.

Chapter Twenty-Eight

The following day, Wednesday, was very busy, just as Susannah had hoped. They cleaned, they cooked, they baked, and then Jane's Robert Malcomb arrived for supper. All the fuss was just for him.

After proper introductions and plenty of blushing, the four of them gathered around the table to eat the meal that Jane had prepared.

"Robert, I don't mean to brag on Jane, but she did almost all the cooking for supper tonight. She's a wonderful baker and that bread you're heaping butter on right now came from Jane's expert hand at it."

Robert looked over at Jane and gave a lopsided smile. "It's mighty good, Miss Jane. I don't believe I've ever had bread so tasty. And I do like a good piece of bread." He nodded slowly as he took another big bite of the bread.

Jane blushed deeply, but managed to smile back at him. "Thank you, kindly Mr. Robert. I'm pleased as punch you like it."

Lucas chuckled. "I'll be sad to see her go, that's for sure. Not that my Susie can't bake a good loaf of bread, but Miss Jane here is a true gem in the kitchen." He winked at Susannah and she smiled back with a raised eyebrow.

Just as she turned back to her plate, Jane dropped her fork. When it clattered to the floor, her knife followed it and almost stabbed Robert's hand as he had leaned down to pick up her fork.

"Well, golly gee, I'm so sorry. Stabbing you wasn't in my plan for the night, Mr. Robert." The blush returned to Janes face in a deeper tone this time. "Thank you." She gazed at him sideways as she took the utensils from him.

Susannah rose to bring a clean fork and knife to the clumsy girl. She didn't miss a beat and didn't comment on the incident.

"You're quite welcome. I'm glad you dropped the fork instead of me." Robert looked at her with a flicker in his eyes. "I'm usually the one who has to get clean utensils to finish a meal. We're very much alike, I think."

Jane smiled at him and nodded. "I doubt that, but thanks for saying so. I'm actually pretty clumsy. I drop everything."

Robert laughed again and continued eating. "As long as you don't forget how to make suppers like this, we'll be a perfect match, Miss Jane."

Jane's smile couldn't be suppressed. The praise from Robert had opened her up. Susannah looked at Lucas and gave a quick nod—her communication to him that she'd been right. He raised an eyebrow back and smiled.

Jane had no confidence and her self-esteem had been badly damaged. Her parents had criticized her incessantly and made their opinions about her shortcomings well known. Jane was embarrassed to be seen in their small community. Building her up and helping her believe in herself had been a challenge, but Robert had managed to accomplish more in a few short moments than she had in many weeks.

Thank You, Lord.

"Is anyone interested in dessert on the porch? We have pie, apple and berry, I think. Is that right, Jane?"

"Yes, that's what we have. I prefer the apple pie, myself." She stood and took Robert's empty plate with hers to the kitchen. "I can do the dishes later."

The small group gathered together on the porch and enjoyed pie and easy, casual conversation. Robert's obvious infatuation with Jane made the evening a sweet and precious one for Susannah.

"Well, I suppose I'd best be getting out of here and let you folks get some sleep." Robert stood and turned to Jane. "If it's acceptable to you, Miss Jane, I'd like to call on you tomorrow afternoon."

"That would be lovely. I'll be looking forward to it." Jane smiled at Robert and this time, she didn't blush.

Susannah and Lucas stood and walked with Robert down the steps and into the yard. "So glad you could join us tonight, Robert." Susannah gave him a quick hug and headed back to the porch were Jane waited.

"He really is nice," the girl murmured.

It made Susannah want to sigh in relief, knowing that once again she had made the match work. In this case, it was obvious this couple would have a long and happy life together. That made Susannah thankful for what she did.

There had been only three occasions where the matches had not turned out well, but that meant she still had a great success record. Except it never got any easier, and Susie never allowed herself to get complacent. Not when other people's happiness was at stake. So every time still felt like the first, with a prayer in her heart that it would work out.

Over the next few days, Susannah and Jane talked more than usual since their time together was coming to an end. Jane had been there long enough and was more than ready to run a household. Robert stopped by daily for the rest of his time there. The two went for horse rides and strolls where they could talk and get to know each other better. Most every night the four had supper together in the Jessup's big dining room.

And sure enough, the next Saturday brought them another wedding. Jane had hemmed her nicest dress and Susannah had given her flowers collected from the garden. The ceremony was short and sweet, the new married couple blushing madly as they held hands. Before Jane and her husband left that night, she made sure to hug Mrs. Jessup tightly.

"Thank you for taking me in. For all you did for me. I don't know what I'd have done if not for you." Tears filled Jane's eyes but she quickly recovered. "I don't mean to cry. This is a happy occasion!"

"Happy, indeed. And Jane, you'd have done fine without me. You had it in you all along." Susannah reached out and took her hand. "Never forget that."

Jane nodded, then paused. "Is this what it was like for you, when you first came out here?"

Susannah wasn't certain she'd been asked that before. Biting her tongue, the woman considered it. "I didn't have anyone here to help me in the beginning. That's why I do this, to help other girls now. Because I'm very happy, Jane, and I want you all to be happy as well."

"Do you ever get tired of this? The silly, naïve girls and all those weddings?"

With a shake of her head, Susannah answered, "I do not, not one bit. Every one of you girls brings me such joy. And who doesn't love a wedding?" Chuckling, she pulled back and allowed the young bride to be pulled up into the wagon. "Your last assignment, Mrs. Malcomb, is to write to me. I won't have you forgetting about what you've learned here. I won't have you forget us."

The girl beamed. "I wouldn't dare! I'll write you a letter tomorrow, Mrs. Jessup. I could never thank you enough."

"We could never thank you enough," her new husband corrected her and they shared sheepish smiles. "Come visit us soon," he added and their entwined hands waved as one as they left.

She backed up, sighing as the last weight lifted off her shoulders. It wasn't a heavy one, but it surely kept her grounded. That sort of weight kept her focused and centered. And now, while it felt good, Susannah wondered if she would float away.

Just as she wondered this, Lucas's arms wrapped around her, and she leaned into him. He would keep her feet on the ground. The sun was setting and their day was coming to an end. Her body was exhausted after the busy day with the wedding, but her mind was lively and thinking back to the young girl's question. What was it like in the beginning, being a mail order bride and coming to marry a man she didn't know?

Chapter Twenty-Nine

Colorado Springs, Colorado; 1872

It was just after Christmas, and there had been a big storm. Tired of Boston and knowing that her poor, hard-working parents could do nothing for her, she had decided to strike out and try for an adventure.

With so little promise for a good future, she thought she'd take it into her hands with the help of God, and go somewhere new. After a tearful goodbye, she'd boarded a train.

The ride was only supposed to take four days to reach Colorado, but the big storm had slowed them down. An avalanche kept them from passing through the mountains for a week before the way was cleared, and two weeks later she arrived in the freezing Colorado Springs.

Her city boots were not made for a place like this. She'd grown up with snow in the winter, but it seemed different than this. She was unprepared for brutally cold weather like this.

Her feet chilled as she'd looked around the station,

wondering what she was supposed to do now. Doubts had overcome her mind with the travel delays, worried that the man she was supposed to marry—a Mr. Lucas Jessup—had given up on her. He had mentioned it would be a bit of a ride to his house, since it was supposed to be outside of Colorado Springs. A place called Rocky Ridge.

"What does that even mean?" she had muttered, stamping her feet to pull some warmth into them. "How can someone live outside a town? You're always in one, aren't you?"

She waved away the puffs of smoke caused by her deep breaths, and carefully climbed down the steps. For a moment Susannah had thought it would help her to see further around her, but now that she was on ground level, all she could see were horses and strangers and buildings around her. Rolling her eyes at her silly decision, the young woman considered going back to the station.

Except there was nothing there for her, unless she wanted to try and turn back for Boston. But that train was going further west, and she'd have to wait a good long while before finding a train that was headed back where she'd come from. Clinging to her heavy bag, Susannah tried to decide what she should do next.

"Dear Lord, please don't let me freeze," she mumbled.

One of the buildings across the street had smoke streaming from the chimney. Drawing a closer look, it was discovered that there were people going in and out of the doors, laughing and talking happily. As the doors swung back and forth, the young lost woman smelled something that drew her to the place. She had to see what they offered.

"Mmm…" Susannah stepped through the front door and stood still as she took it all in.

Whatever this place was called, she realized immediately it was nothing like home. If anything, it looked like one of the saloons she knew many men would wander into in the evenings. But, Susannah pondered, there were a few women there, and they were decently dressed. Certainly, this meant it was an acceptable place?

Dropping her gaze as several people stared at her, Susannah made it across the room and sat at a small round table that was unoccupied, and set her bag at her feet. It was a cozy little place packed with people. Even in a decent place in Boston, it wouldn't be so full. Perhaps, her stomach rumbled, the food was good.

"Or just warmer than outside," she murmured, and glanced around to see how she should order. Would someone come see her, or did she need to find someone behind the counter? Just as she was wondering about what to do, a large man covered in a filthy apron arrived at her side.

"What can we get you today?" he grumbled loudly.

For a minute she gaped. "Um…soup?" It was impossible to know with a certainty what they served. Every place should have soup in the winter, shouldn't they? She supposed she could ask what they have, but soup would warm her up on a day like today.

The man muttered something, but he had a strong accent and was already wandering away to the counter. Biting her lip, Susannah felt her heart pound loudly as she was reminded again that she was in a strange place surrounded by strange people.

Her parents had asked her what would compel her to

do such a thing, leave a familiar home for the unknown. At the time, she couldn't answer them. It made little sense in any form. But somehow, she just felt that she had needed to do this. She had to. Even if, right now, she was doubting her decision with all she had.

"Well now, isn't that a friendly face." She looked up in surprise to find someone talking to her. "Are you waiting for anyone in particular, little lady?"

His tone was as friendly as the smile he wore, but there was something in his eyes that made Susannah put up her guard. No one was watching her now. Tapping a heel on the hard plank floor, she hesitantly turned back to the man. "I think so."

Only then did it occur to her that she should have been more assured. Dropping her gaze, she tried to think of something to say to get him to leave, not wanting to spend the afternoon with a stranger. Especially not this one. He was dirty, he smelled very bad, and she didn't like the way he was looking at her.

There were enough men like him in the city, too, and she had hoped they had all been left behind in the dust and crowds. Biting the inside of her cheek, the young woman glanced around in hopes of finding someone there who might pull this man away from her. But they were all ignoring the two of them now.

Patting her damp hair self-consciously, Susannah tried to find something to ask the gentleman to go away. But he leaned over the table, his eyes on her. "You're awful pretty. Too pretty to be alone. I can take you back to my place, if you like. How about we leave now?"

Startled, she felt the hair on the back of her neck raise as she swallowed hard. "I, um…no, I told you, I'm waiting for someone—"

But his smile was fading as he stood, gripping her bag as he reached out and took her by the elbow. It was a hard hold, and she knew immediately she wouldn't be able to escape it. "They'll find us at my place. Don't worry, little lady."

"Jamison Minks, the young lady said no."

A voice came from nearby the counter, and she dropped her gaze, biting her lip. Now the folks decided to pay attention. She could feel the eyes just as surely as she felt the blush crawling up her face. The man that held her whirled around, nearly tipping her off balance.

"Don't you talk to me like that, you—"

Susannah cried out, feeling herself falling as the man went down. Her heart jumped in her throat and she tried to prepare herself for the hard ground. But just in time, she was yanked in the other direction and the next time she opened her eyes, the ground was still steady below her feet with a gentler touch on her shoulders.

Carefully squinting around, Susannah swallowed hard and hid her shaking hands in her skirts. Most of the folks had turned back to their food, now that most of the excitement was over. She was annoyed that each of them had uselessly stood by when she needed assistance.

At her feet, she found the despicable man, apparently his name was Jamison Minks, lying there, out cold. There was blood trickling down his nose and drool hanging off his bottom lip.

Speechless, she glanced up to find a tall man there who dropped his arms from her and took a step back so that they could appraise one another. Tall, and of a good stature, she noticed immediately. Dark unruly hair and a firm dark gaze. She saw the sparkle of a badge on his chest but barely noticed it once she saw the scar.

Lucas Jessup had told her about it, warning her that she wouldn't be finding herself a pretty husband. The man had faced outlaws and other dangerous folk from all over in his days as a Texas Ranger, and had the marks to show it.

Susannah had prepared herself, thinking that perhaps a scar would make her husband appear debonair. But now, in her state of shock, she marveled at the fact that his serious expression only made the scar appear more intense, stark white against his tan frame. All she could think was that Jamison Minks had to be a fool to try and stand up against a man like this.

As she decided between cowering or fainting, the man made the decision. "Howdy, ma'am, and welcome to the west." He offered a tight smile as he took off his hat and set it on the table. "Would you take a seat? I'll take him out, and I'll be right with you." Without waiting for her reply, Lucas Jessup grabbed Minks and took him outside to the street.

So much for first impressions. Surely her legs wouldn't hold much longer, so Susannah found herself slipping back into her seat. Eyes flitting around, she saw her bag still lying on the floor and hurriedly snatched it up, brushing away the dust.

"Coffee cake?"

Jumping, Susannah looked up with wide eyes to find Lucas there again, holding two plates in one hand, and two glasses in the other. There was a patch of snow on one shoulder, and he was giving her a sheepish smile.

"Oh, well…of, of course," she stammered, failing to find anything else to say. "Thank you."

He set them down and glanced at the chair, hesitating. It was only a moment, however, and Susannah wondered if she had imagined it. By the time he sat down and turned to her, the man's facial impression was impassive as he carefully set the plates, forks, and glasses in their proper places.

"I'm Lucas. Lucas Jessup," he stated calmly. "I believe I've been looking for you for some time now." And his eyes caught hers as though she'd fallen into a trap. Those eyes of his were so clear, not in color but in purpose and faith.

Though her lips parted, it took a minute for Susannah to find her voice. She had been worried he wouldn't know her, that he wouldn't find her. But he did. He had found her. How?

He was identifiable by the scar, but she had no distinctive characteristics. Shaking the confusion from her mind, Susannah told herself to pull together. Nodding, she offered a small smile. "I thought it was you. I'm Susannah Tumlin. And I'm terribly sorry, but there was an avalanche, and we were stuck on the train for days. I wasn't sure what to think, if you would come back or just forget about the whole thing. I didn't know if you'd know about the delay or not."

Shaking his head, he picked up his fork. "You don't forget or give up something like this. It's a bit of a ride, but I've made it every day in case you showed up. So, I'm mighty glad you finally did."

"Oh." She was taken aback at his efforts. "I'm terribly sorry for your trouble."

He took a sip of the drink. Hot coffee, she realized finally, and hurriedly sipped hers as well. Warmth immediately spread from her throat to her fingertips. "Don't be. Out here, nothing comes easy and I would expect nothing less. I'm only sorry I wasn't here sooner."

"What do you mean?"

Pointing behind him, he gestured towards the porch. "Minks." Surprised, she realized she had already forgotten about the other man. Settled comfortably in her seat, there was something about the confident, calm tone of Lucas's voice and his steady gaze that made her feel secure and safe.

"He's been plenty of trouble but nobody could prove it. I've tried a few times whenever he stops by Rocky Ridge. This is enough to keep him in a cell for a few days, and let him stew until we figure something out."

Swallowing, she nodded but didn't know what else to say. Their conversation wandered as he asked her about Boston and the train ride, and then as she asked him about the area and his life. Eventually, they finished up and he took her to the next street over to the boarding house where she would stay until they were married.

She wanted to know more about him, but the last few hours had been trying. Though she'd spent the last two weeks basically alone, she still craved some time to herself. She wasn't sure what came next, but she'd deal with it no matter what.

Chapter Thirty

"So, here we are. The Main Street Boarding House. It's not fancy like what you'd find back in Boston, but I hope it'll meet your needs." Lucas opened the door and stood back to let her go inside before him.

He walked up to the desk and tipped his hat. "Hello there. This lady here needs a place to stay. I talked to Mr. Talmadge about it just the other day. Miss Susannah Tumlin."

"Yes, I have the name here. And you'll be picking up the bill, I assume, sir."

"Yes, I will."

"Good. Good. Sign here in the registry, then, please." The clerk turned to look at Susannah. "Shall I show you to your room now, ma'am?"

Susannah hesitated as she clutched her carpet bag in front of her. There was a dusty smell to her, and she knew she had to look rumpled at the very least. But she wasn't sure what would happen next, what she should do. As they stood there, she tried to find the right way to ask him.

"Should I hurry and put my bag away, or will I see

you tomorrow?" She bit her lip and looked at him. Standing on that first step, now they stood eye to eye.

His scar stood out prominently high on his cheek-bone, and she wondered if it had hurt badly.

"I really should return to Rocky Ridge," he admitted. "I have Old Jerry in a cell back in town, sleeping off a few pints and have to make sure he doesn't hurt himself. But I'll be here tomorrow morning if you don't mind a late breakfast?"

Trying to quell the nerves, she nodded quickly. "Yes. Yes, of course." Biting her lip, she watched him tip his hat and turn away. The man never looked back as he crossed the room and stepped out the door. There was a large window in front and she saw him step across the street, and finally mount a large horse. Soon, he and the horse were gone.

She turned to the clerk and smiled. "Yes, I'd be happy to see my room now, please."

The man nodded and stepped around the desk and to her side. He stuck out his hand and took her bag. "I'll take this for you, ma'am."

"Thank you."

"Now we're not formal or fancy around here. The kitchen serves supper at five o'clock. Be sure to not miss it or you'll go hungry. Tonight is roast chicken and vegetables. The cook is pretty good, so hopefully you won't go hungry."

"Sounds lovely. Thank you again." Susannah followed him to her room and was thankful they were finally there.

As soon as she was alone inside, she stretched out on the bed, still wearing her boots and her cloak. The room was chilly, but she was too tired to build a fire. She'd do that in just a minute.

Finally, she opened her eyes and realized she'd been asleep for almost an hour. She jumped up to check the time as she didn't want to be late for supper. She'd had a little bite to eat at the restaurant earlier, but she felt her stomach grumble. There was a few minutes to spare and she let out a sigh of relief.

She got up and made a fire in the small fireplace. Thankful the wood box was full, she thought about her next few days and what they might bring. Changes, for sure.

She needed time to fully accept that she was actually here in Colorado and had met the man who would become her husband. For better or for worse.

Chapter Thirty-One

As promised, he returned the following morning. Lucas showed her around town after borrowing a buggy. There was an old couple he knew, who kept bees and showed her around and gave her a small jar of their finest honey. It was delicious and more pure than anything she had tasted before.

Just as they were returning to town, there was a brawl that had spilled out into the streets from the nearby saloon.

Immediately Lucas had straightened up and handed her the reins after pulling the horse to a stop. "I need to take care of this seeing as there's no other lawman around," he said and left her. Susannah stared, barely recalling that he'd mentioned the sheriff in this town did very little when he was drunk and even less when he was sober.

Holding the reins, she wondered how he was going to stop them just as she learned the answer. Lucas shouted and waved his arms to get their attention, but they hardly noticed. Susannah bit her lip in concern and then waited for his next move.

"Pardon me." He tapped the nearest one on his shoulder and when the man looked, Lucas swung a sharp right hook into his jaw. The man went down like a sack of flour.

She gasped out loud and stared at the fallen figure. But it didn't stop Lucas as it didn't stop the other men. Immediately they carried on the fight, fists swinging and feet dancing. Another went down, leaving one man standing besides Lucas.

"Now listen. You just go on home now. Your friends here will wake up and get on their way, too. Unless the sheriff comes along. Maybe he'll take 'em in, maybe he won't. Either way, you'll be in the clear if you leave now."

The man turned and walked away with slumped shoulders and a slight limp.

Susannah stared incredulously, and couldn't find anything to say when Lucas returned. The fight was finished, but his knuckles were bleeding.

"Here we go," he murmured, and started them off again as though nothing had happened. They were quiet all the way back to the boarding house as she tried to find something to say, but she couldn't. Her throat only tightened as he led her to the doors. "I'm sorry you had to see that," Lucas glanced away. "They were little rowdy."

"I see," she murmured. "Well, you need a cold cloth on those knuckles."

That made him smile. "Aww, they'll be fine. I'll be sure to stick them in a pile of snow now and again," Lucas offered. "I'll be back tomorrow. I'll pick you up at mid-day?"

She nodded, and he was gone. Susannah decided he must not get in fights all that often, and decided to let it go. She wasn't sure what the life of a sheriff was like in these parts. Back home, there was more than a hand-ful of lawmen, so order was easier to keep.

When he returned the next day, they had lunch at the same restaurant where they'd met. The place she'd needed help with the notorious Mr. Minks. She sat across the table from him fidgeting a bit, hoping he didn't notice. At first, their conversation was halting and formal, but they ignored it as they started planning a wedding date.

He led her outside and around the corner to where he'd left the borrowed buggy. He helped her in and moved around to sit beside her. "I'll take the long way back to the boarding house so you can see more of the lovely area you've come to live in."

She nodded and smiled, looking forward to the time to see her surroundings better. More than that, she looked forward to spending more time with Lucas. She realized she like him and wanted to know more about him.

"So, I'll talk to the pastor tomorrow," Lucas promised her, and shared another one of those brief smiles. They continued down the road that took them to the edge of town.

She nodded, trying not to shiver as they stuck to the path near the mountains. "Good, that would be lovely. Hopefully the sun will shine."

Overhead, an eagle cried out, flapping its wings. "I'm sure it—" But he never finished the sentence as he suddenly gripped her arm tightly as he stared into the trees. The man's entire body had stiffened, and Susannah looked around for trouble.

"Is something wrong?"

"Shh!"

The man appeared to listen for something, but she couldn't hear a thing. His grip only tightened, and she didn't recognize the strange expression on his face. Her heart pounded in her chest as she tried to understand what was going on, but she didn't. It was a strange place, with a strange man, who was acting strange. "They're coming."

"What? Who?" Squinting, she looked for something and her breath caught. But it was nature, the trees. What was there to see? She swallowed, her heartbeat only growing louder. "Um, Lucas? My arm—you're hurting me. Let go. Please?"

But he didn't appear to hear her, as he pulled her out of the buggy and started tugging her downhill, crouching and watching his steps as he went. An inkling of fear trickled down her spine and her chin quivered. "Keep your head low, and stop talking. We'll cross the river so they lose our scent. Faster, Ralph, or—"

"Who's Ralph?" Her shaky breath frosted in front of her and she ran into it at the pace he was trying to pull her. Though Susannah protested, Lucas was much stronger and was practically dragging her. "Lucas Jessup! No, stop this!" Being gentle wasn't going to get her what she wanted apparently, so she tried more loudly. "Stop!"

It did the trick. Lucas stepped awkwardly on a rock and they both stumbled. He caught them just in time, and the man's eyes widened as he looked like he just woke up. With a haggard expression, Lucas gaped at her looking as confused as she was.

Pursing her lips, she yanked her arm free, certain that his fingers would leave a mark. Without saying anything, Susannah turned and started walking. The town was just over the hill, and she was returning to it. Glancing at her hands, she found they were shaking and felt it all the way to her chilled bones.

"Susannah? Susannah!"

The shock must have taken some time to wear off. Or whatever it was. All she knew was that it had scared her, and she hadn't liked it one bit. Wrapping her arms around herself, she ignored Lucas and asked the Lord if He was making a joke of her, or if she had understood Him wrong.

"Wait." A second later, his arm grabbed hers and she flinched, pulling away. He let her go.

Susannah opened her mouth to say something, but that cold look in his eyes from a moment ago, that had terrified her, and it was all she could picture. As she tried to step away, Susannah slipped and fell in the snow.

Lucas knelt to lend a hand. "Here, let me—"

"Don't touch me," she ordered firmly. Shivering, she tightened her grip around herself and looked away. Taking a deep breath, the young woman searched for something to say though she could feel the cold wetness from the snow creeping through her clothes.

"Miss Susannah, let me help you."

Biting her tongue, she refused to give in. "No. You scared me, and I don't want you touching me. I don't know this Ralph person and I don't see a river anywhere around here. So..."

The hand he had opened up to her suddenly tightened into a fist which formed a knot in her stomach immediately. A sudden dread filled her, wondering if this is where she would die. If he would beat her senseless. But Lucas sighed and sat down in the snow beside her, not caring about the dampness either.

"Joshua Ralph," he told her, "is my friend. He's another Ranger. This, um, sort of incident has only happened once before. I have heard that others have... experienced this as well. Rangers live a difficult, dangerous life that's hard to leave behind. Even mentally. I don't know what it is, but I hear that it could be anything that sends me back. A smell, a touch, the sound of a gunshot. When it happened before it wasn't quite like that."

She scoffed. "You make it sound so simple."

He didn't smile. "I guess we don't always have a choice about what comes our way. You face it head on, come what may."

After a minute, Susannah bit her lip and glanced at him. There was another look in his eyes, a musing one that made him look older. He hadn't liked what had happened to himself either. It didn't matter, she decided, and she focused on his eyes now instead of his scar. "I like that," she said finally.

"My parents told me that once," he sighed.

Nodding, she looked down at the space between them and wondered why it suddenly felt so spacious. "It doesn't happen often?"

"Only once before. I woke up in the middle of the night, listening for an ambush."

Then he was silent. It surprised her that he didn't try to make promises, to tell her that it would never happen again. Most would do that, even if it wasn't true. Lucas proclaimed honesty was a virtue, and it seemed he certainly kept to it.

Could she? Biting her lip, Susannah glanced around. It was rather pretty, she admitted, and hoped that Rocky Ridge looked like this as well. He promised they would go there soon, only that it was without a boarding house or hotel yet which is why she stayed there. Biting her lip, Susannah felt herself giving in.

"All right. I'm ready to go back," she announced, and pulled herself out of the pile of snow. It was difficult, but she refused any help as she climbed onto her two feet and shook the damp powder from her clothes.

Lucas straightened up beside her and they started walking together back to the buggy.

It was quiet, but decidedly peaceful. Susannah used the time to weigh her decision. In two days they were supposed to be wed. Was this a life she could promise herself to? It wasn't what she had expected. But then again, nothing was what she expected.

The thing was, she realized when they reached town, she already had an answer. Boston was already a place in her past, and Colorado was exactly where she wanted to be. Whether it was Colorado Springs or Rocky Ridge or somewhere new, Susannah could feel it in her heart that she had to be here. Though she questioned the Lord's way, she would still listen and be obedient.

"Would you eat supper with me?"

Her eyes flickered towards the setting sun. "It's getting late, and I think you should go. But don't be late on Friday," she added when he started to turn away. When Lucas glanced back, she managed a hesitant smile. "And bring me those flowers you told me about, will you? I'd like to wear one in my hair."

Though his lips didn't move, she saw his eyes crinkle up. They turned soft, deep as damp earth after a good rain. Pain was there, Susannah noticed, but so was hope. "I'll do just that. Friday, then."

She nodded and as usual, she watched him walk away. Her chest grew tight, and she wondered if that was normal. It would take a few years, but Susannah would discover the answer was yes, it was normal. Even though Lucas swore the job of watching over their town and area was safe, it still invited recklessness and occasional danger.

Being a lawman's wife might take some getting used to.

Chapter Thirty-Two

The young bride was reminded that it might take patience to be married to a man like Lucas on her wedding day. She'd put on her nicest dress and pulled out the veil her mother had given her. Upon her arrival at the little chapel, she was met by the pastor and they waited quietly together for Lucas.

Her husband-to-be was an hour late, and she'd decided it wasn't meant to be. He wasn't coming. Not sure what she'd do next, she knew God would help her figure something out. Worry and frustration and finally anger had ruined a day she'd hoped would be a happy one. She was putting on her coat and hat when the large doors burst open and two stragglers arrived.

Two men, one keeping the other one up. They'd been talking loudly but fell silent as they stepped inside and found her blocking their way. She blinked against the sunlight they brought in behind them, unable to tell if either was the man she'd been waiting for. She took a step backward.

"Susie?" It was the first time he'd called her that,

and it made her heart pound. So he was the one being kept on his feet by the other man. "Ralph, this is Susie."

Clearing her throat, Susannah gave them measured looks. It appeared they were both injured. The other man he called Ralph might have been keeping her man on his feet, but he was favoring a shoulder. She could feel their grins.

"You're an hour late to your own wedding, and you want to introduce me to someone?" She'd been raised to be polite, but she'd had enough of this. Shaking her head, she started to button her coat. "This is ridiculous. I can't believe anyone would be so—"

"There was a situation. We would have been here on time if we could have been. You wouldn't leave me at the altar, would you?" Lucas sounded more jovial and it made her wonder if he was drunk.

"Certainly looks like you were leaving me," she snapped and then took a deep breath as she straightened her skirts. "We had an agreement and it looks like you changed your mind. I would have preferred more clear communication."

Lucas tugged himself free of his friend, Ralph, and put out an arm. He swayed, and grabbed for a bench that he leaned against. Clearing his throat, the man took a slow and deep breath. "You're correct, we did have an agreement. And I apologize for not being able to be here on time, as I had told you. My good friend from the Rangers, Joshua Ralph, arrived by train and I wanted him to be here for this special occasion."

Ralph smiled sheepishly, and closed the doors behind them with his good arm. Her gaze drifted back to Lucas where she found his left pant leg was slightly ripped, and his leg bleeding. So that's what she had smelled.

"We were on our way over here, however, when we came across an old…"

"He's not a friend." Ralph shook his head. "Not quite an enemy either."

"Foe?"

"Er, acquaintance?"

"Yeah, that might work."

Susannah cleared her throat and Lucas continued. "Thing is, he was cheating some men out of their money and they were trying to have a shootout right by the station. We tried to talk to them, but they wouldn't listen."

Ralph backed up the story. "Marius McConnel was supposed to be rotting in a Texas prison cell. Pardon the language, ma'am, but we couldn't stand by and let anyone else get hurt. Well, besides Lucas. But he always was foolhardy." The two of them chuckled as though it were an inside joke. But stopped when they looked at her face. "I'll go see the pastor." Ralph stepped away to give them a minute.

As she tried to process her thoughts and emotions, Lucas attempted to straighten up. He was dressed in a suit she hadn't seen before, one with a nice vest and jacket. It was a shame that the pants were ruined. And why did his friend use that word, foolhardy? Did this mean it would be normal, finding her husband staggering home whenever he felt like causing trouble?

"Susannah." He limped forward and took one of her hands. She didn't protest, but she didn't look him in the eye either. Even though she knew it mattered to him and he tried to make their gazes meet. "Please, Susannah Tumlin. I would never have tried to… I was trouble, as a Ranger, I'll admit. I ran into enemy fire whenever I liked, just because I could. But that's not that way any more."

A knot formed in her throat. "Are you sure about that?"

His hand squeezed hers. "I left the service because I didn't want to die young. I left so I could buy some land, and start a family. They asked me to be sheriff for Rocky Ridge because they knew I would do my best and hardest to protect the town…and the nearby areas when necessary," he added after a second and took a deep breath. "This happens sometimes. Not usually so often, but it does happen."

"Is that what you want?" she asked dully. "To come home to a family, all banged up?"

He frowned. "Of course not. I told you, my family comes first. You will come first. If…if it matters this much, if you really want," he took a deep breath, "I'll quit."

Her heart skipped a beat as she looked up to meet his gaze. She searched his eyes and as usual, found truth. He meant it. And for a minute, Susannah wanted to say yes, to accept this bargain and ensure his safety. But as her mouth opened, she knew she couldn't do that to him. Lucas liked his job, and she had already accepted his way of life by coming to him.

"Don't," she said in resignation. "Just promise to be more careful. And on time to other important engagements."

He grinned, showing off those sharp cheekbones of his. She was fairly certain, even in this lighting, he had a bruise forming on the right side, right beside that scar. His unruly hair flopped into his face, but it glinted in the light with oils that he must have tried to use to flatten it down. It made her chest tight but she tried to loosen her insides and relax. "I can do that," he assured her, and put out his arm.

First, she took off her hat and then her jacket. Then she rolled her eyes at his arm and wrapped it around her neck, offering herself as a crutch to help him down the aisle. At first the man protested, but one stern look shut him up. It made her smile as Lucas grumbled under his breath, and she decided they would make things work out just fine.

Joshua Ralph cheered them on, and took over for her so that she could stand across from her fiancé. As the pastor spoke, Lucas slipped a hand into his jacket pocket, and drew forth a slightly wilted blue columbine flower. It was as pretty as he had told her, and she smiled, sticking it in her hair to the side of her temple.

"I now pronounce you man and wife," the pastor proclaimed. "Good sir, you may kiss your bride."

And Lucas did. It made Susannah blush bright red, but she immediately discovered that kissing was just as delightful as she'd heard, and the way he touched her around the waist was nice, too. Maybe this would work out, after all.

Chapter Thirty-Three

Rocky Ridge, Colorado; 1882

"You were a mess," Susannah giggled as they settled in for the evening. "Why, I'm still amazed sometimes that I actually said yes. You were terrible, Lucas. No girl in her right mind would have ever gone through with it."

She heard him chuckle as he made sure the fire was out. "That's why I knew I couldn't marry just any girl, of course." Then he came up behind her and kissed her cheek, catching her by surprise. It made her jump, furious for not having heard him. He was still as stealthy as a mountain cat.

"That's why I got you."

Though she swatted at him, he was already out of reach pulling the last of the curtains together. Susannah put the towels away in the cupboard, but paused when she touched the soft crocheted blanket in the back. Immediately she knew what it was. It was a small blanket, one that had never been finished. Susannah froze, having thought that it had been thrown out long ago.

Lucas said something, but she didn't hear him. Eventually he walked over, and found what she was staring at. Reaching in, her husband pulled out the unfinished blanket, and they stared at it together.

In the silence, it reminded them too loudly of what they didn't have. What they would never have, Susannah corrected herself. Something gnawed inside at her heart, bringing back pain and fear that she thought had been put away for good. "Where did it come from?" she whispered.

"I thought we had passed everything along."

The few things she had started to work on from time to time—little blankets and hats and shoes—in the hope that soon a baby would be growing inside her had been given to young mothers who actually could use such items.

Not trusting her voice, she nodded. But then, Susannah reprimanded herself, they were over this. The woman reminded herself of the happiness and joy she had already. Lucas tossed the yarn over to the table, out of her view. Before she could turn to it, he was guiding her to the bedroom with the lowly lit lantern. "I'll pass it along to Mrs. Ruthers tomorrow, I think. She has another one on the way."

She already had six children. Susannah shook her head and sighed, leaning into her husband as they made their way into the bedroom. It was big and it was spacious, very comfortable with their separate chests and large canopied bed. Susannah was blessed with so much, why did she think she needed anything more?

"We have children," she mused finally, once she had changed for the night. "Don't we? Not the pigs, of course. Young ladies, eyes bright and hopeful with so much to learn. We just get them for a shorter amount of time, really."

Lucas smiled after a moment, and nodded. Their eyes met, and it started her heart as it always did. She could see all of him when they looked at one another, and Susannah knew every part of his soul.

"You're right," he said. "Mrs. Ruthers and her brood will never compare to what we accomplish."

It made her giggle. "Oh, be nice. And I'm sure she'll appreciate the blanket. Perhaps I'll finish it for her first?" She inhaled deeply, falling into her pillow. "I really am lucky, you know."

"Oh really?" He snuffed the lantern out and pulled her close. Though they were growing older, some things never changed, and that's what Susannah loved. He had changed over the last few years as well, growing quieter in many ways but much sillier. He liked to laugh more than he wanted to search out trouble, which was a change she loved.

Had she grown? Susannah yawned and wondered this even as her husband kissed her brow, brushing back a strand of hair that had escaped her braid. She brushed her fingertips across his jawline almost absently, wondering how he was always so warm. Closing her eyes, Susannah Tumlin Jessup curled close to her husband, and knew she had everything she needed right there beside her.

* * * * *

ELEANOR AND MATTHEW

Chapter One

Boston, Massachusetts; 1877

Eleanor sighed. The faint smell of baking pies wafted past her nose, their fragrance weakened by the pies having cooled. It was a cold, damp spring day, and business was slow. People didn't go to the open market when it was this soggy out unless they had to.

The weather wasn't having a favorable effect on Eleanor's wares, either. Usually she'd have a few days to sell her baked goods before they were too stale, but her rolls and pies seemed to soak up the moisture in the air. Perhaps it was just the dreary fog weighing Eleanor down, along with the warm coats, smart hats, and necessary offerings of every other man, woman and stall in the market.

"Slow morning, isn't it?" Mrs. Kent, who worked at the vegetable stand next door, yelled over. Not many people were purchasing her wares, either.

"You're telling me. I don't know how many more days like this I can take." Eleanor shook her head with a frown.

"Aye. This weather's a devil to business."

Eleanor sighed again. Mrs. Kent might be losing sales, but she didn't have as much to lose as Eleanor. Her husband was a farmer, and very much alive. Even if they were low on money, they could live off their farm—at least for a while. Eleanor didn't have that luxury. If she didn't sell pies and all her other baked goods, she might not have a roof over her head.

Eleanor Trimble, at the tender age of twenty-four, had become a widow. Influenza had taken her husband, John, only months after their baby had been stillborn. That had been a year ago, and since then she'd been selling baked goods at the market. Eleanor's pies were good, but it's hard to build a life on selling baked goods in a market out in the open with just the sky above.

Picking up her knife, Eleanor sliced into a rhubarb pie.

"Can't let all this go to waste, now can we?" She handed a large slice to Mrs. Kent.

Once a pie was started, it simply had to be finished. By the time the market closed, Eleanor and Mrs. Kent had eaten a whole pie between them.

Eleanor shook her head as she packed her unsold goods into the hand-cart she used to trek to and from the market. She'd eaten more pie than she'd sold, today. Eleanor really couldn't take any more days like this.

The scene at home was not encouraging, either. As soon as Eleanor walked through the door, her mother put her hands on her hips and looked at her expectantly. Eleanor pulled the day's meager earnings from her pocket and dropped the coins into her mother's hand.

"One pie and a dozen cookies," she said shortly, not

waiting for her mother to reply before heading to the kitchen. Mother followed her anyway, incensed.

"What kind of day's work is this?" she scolded. "I slave here all day, taking in laundry to make a few pennies, and this is the help I get from you? Ungrateful girl. We don't have to support you, you know. You're a grown woman. You've got to contribute to the family like a grown woman."

Eleanor put away her left-over, unsold pies with her back to her ranting mother, mouthing the words of her lecture along with her. She'd heard this litany many times over.

Shortly after the death of Eleanor's husband, the factory her father worked at had closed. He'd been there for almost forty years. He now spent his days searching for new work, as without his income the family faced the threat of eviction, but he was too old and set in his ways for many employers to be happy with him.

The entire family was scrambling to take up the slack, from the widowed daughter to the youngest sons. The only people who didn't seem concerned about the matter at all were Eleanor's two older brothers, both well situated in trade jobs and both equally disinterested in their poor relations.

"It's bad enough those brothers of yours can't even be bothered to write."

"Much less help out the rest of the family. Yes, Mama, I know." Eleanor slumped wearily. "Trust me. I know."

Christopher came scrambling into the apartment at that moment, interrupting Mother's intensifying ire. He'd been dispatched to the post office to see if there was any mail. There was one letter, but not one that would make Mother happy. It was from Eleanor's friend,

Susannah Jessup, who'd moved out to Colorado to get married.

Eleanor disappeared to the semi-privacy of her bed. She shared a room with her younger brothers, but even when almost everyone was home she wasn't likely to be bothered in there.

My dear Ellie,
I hope this letter finds you in better circumstance than when you last wrote. I have little to report of myself—

A few paragraphs detailing what news a small mountain town provided followed. Susannah wrote with enough detail and regularity about the residents of Rocky Ridge that Eleanor knew exactly who she was talking about, even if she'd never met the new pastor or Matthew Connor in her life. Though Eleanor would have preferred reading more about what happened in Colorado, the subject of Susannah's letter quickly turned to less pleasant things.

It distresses me to hear that life in Boston continues so bad. It makes me realize how few my problems really are in comparison. Even if I have no children, I have a husband and a comfortable home, and I'm not likely to lose either.
Do not think that I write only to brag about my good fortune, for I want to share it with you. I've discussed it with Lucas, and he's agreed that it would be wonderful if you could come to Colorado and stay with us over the summer. I need help around the house, anyway, and a change of

*scenery might be just the thing you need. If noth-
ing else, it would be much harder for your mother
to nag at you in Colorado.*

*If you do choose to come, send a letter back
right away, and we'll know when to expect you.
I took the liberty of outlining an itinerary that
would have you arriving by train at a most rea-
sonable time of day, though traveling overnight
would be required. But you know it is a long journey from Boston to Colorado Springs. It would
be lovely if you could be here for at least part of
the spring.*

Eleanor chuckled. That was just like Susannah, to get
an idea in her head and run away with it. Just like when
she'd decided to move west in the first place.

Setting the letter on the bed, Eleanor took a specula-
tive look at the cheap calendar she'd pinned to the wall.
It was March twentieth and that only gave her a few
days to make a decision and mail a letter to her friends.

"Eleanor!" Mother's voice came shrilling from
downstairs. "Get in here and help with supper!"

Well, it didn't take long to make that decision. As
far as Eleanor was concerned, being in Colorado before
the snow melted was her new priority.

Chapter Two

If she used all the money she'd secreted away, including the sock she'd shoved under the mattress, Eleanor had just enough to buy the necessary train tickets to reach Rocky Ridge, Colorado. She didn't, however, have enough to buy tickets back to Boston. Once she got there, she would be stuck.

Maybe it's actually a good thing, she thought. *If I'm stuck in Colorado, I'll have to start a new life. I won't have another choice.* She'd be taking a page out of Susannah's book, and taking life by the horns. If only she could get rid of the conviction she was going to fail miserably.

Eleanor's family thought she was going to fail miserably, too. Her mother told her over and over again at every opportunity that it was a waste of money. "Better to stay at home and be worthless in a city you know," she said, "than to go be worthless in some miner's hut in the mountains."

Eleanor personally thought that she would gladly have lived in a miner's hut if she didn't have to listen to her mother call her worthless, but luckily she was going someplace much nicer.

It took about three solid days to get from Boston to Rocky Ridge by train, with transfers here and stops of a few hours there. Eleanor was amazed by the changing landscape. The city quickly gave way to small farms, which transformed into rolling, endless plains, which changed yet again into mountains. She stared avidly out the window as the train barreled along, too fascinated to be bored, and the journey was over almost before she knew it.

Susannah and her husband, Lucas, were waiting for her at the train station. Susannah squealed loudly when Eleanor stepped off the train, running over to catch her in a tight hug and subject her to a barrage of chatter.

"Eleanor, I'm so glad to see you! You're the first person from Boston I've seen in almost five years! I haven't even seen Mama since I left. How is Mama, anyway? I told you to check on her while I was gone. I write to her, too, but some things you just can't tell through letters, and I want to know how you think she's doing. And what about Mrs. Kent, the fish woman. Does she still have that cat hanging around her stall? The one with the white tail that tries to steal sardines?"

Behind her, Lucas silently bowed and picked up Eleanor's suitcase. He knew better than to try to ford that flooded river of words.

"This is Lucas, of course." Susannah gestured to him proudly. "He's the sheriff around these parts, but you knew that already. Now you don't have to take my word for it that he's the handsomest lawman this side of Salt Lake City." She beamed as she spoke, prompting a laugh from Eleanor and a calm smile from Lucas.

"Pleased to make your acquaintance, Mr. Jessup," Eleanor said, holding out her hand.

"Yours, as well. And please call me Lucas. No need for formality out here in the mountains." Lucas shook, two quick, efficient shakes before dropping her hand. "Susannah's spoken about you at great length. It will be nice to actually talk to you instead of just talking about you."

"I don't talk all that much." Susannah crossed her arms over her chest with a scowl.

"My love, you talk more than an army of gossiping old women combined," Lucas said drily. "Possibly two armies."

Eleanor laughed again. Susannah had been accurate in describing Lucas, from his handsome looks to his calm, sarcastic temperament. What Susannah hadn't said outright was how much he loved her. His affection was obvious, even to Eleanor's unpracticed eye. Lucas might tease Susannah endlessly, but it was out of playfulness rather than a desire to hurt.

Susannah matched him well. Her replies to his quips might not have always been clever, but she was never without a response. Eleanor had to admit that she'd often been envious of the picture of happiness Susannah had painted in the Colorado Rockies.

The only thing missing was children. On the outside, that didn't seem to be a problem. Eleanor knew that they'd both been disappointed in their inability to have a child, but they seemed to be filling their worlds with each other quite nicely.

"Our buggy's tied up out front," Susannah said, pulling Eleanor through the train station by hand. "Our house is a little bit out of town. It'll take us a while to drive there. The view is wonderful, though. You'll just love these mountains. You can't see anything properly by train, you really have to be out in the open air to appreciate them properly."

The buggy was just barely big enough for three, with the suitcase stowed below. Eleanor tried to shrink herself down as much as possible, but she couldn't hide from the fact that she took up more room than either Susannah or Lucas by themselves. The excitement she'd felt on the train melted away into awkward dread.

The journey was over. Now she had to deal with people knowing who she was and what she looked like, establishing her reputation as the fat widow in a new town.

Eleanor struggled against these somber ideas as the buggy rolled through town. *That's not the way to start a new life,* she thought, and that's what she was here to do. This was a new chapter for Eleanor Trimble. She'd even boldly left her black widow's cap in Boston, cutting away as much of her old life as she could.

Thinking these encouraging thoughts, Eleanor watched the horse trot along at Lucas's command.

Rocky Ridge wasn't a large city by any means. It was only a town, really. They soon left the town proper, the road now edged by forest, hills, and the occasional house. Susannah had been right about the view. No matter what direction Eleanor looked in, blue and purple mountains rose up over the trees. White peaks rose over those, covered with snow that Susannah said never melted. All the etchings and photographs in the world couldn't prepare one for really seeing the Rocky Mountains.

The well-trodden main road split into several smaller

ones, all winding off to different clusters of houses and shacks. Their path followed the left-most one, and fifteen minutes down the road they came to the Jessup family home.

Susannah had said in her letters that Lucas had gone out of his way to make a comfortable home for her. Leaving his bachelor's rooms in town behind, he'd bought some land just outside town and built a house.

It was nothing lavish, but it was large. Clearly the couple had been planning for a big, happy family. There was a bedroom for them to share, another for guests, and more bedrooms for children.

There was a sitting room with a view out the front window, and a spacious kitchen with room for a table and chairs. There was a library and a large dining room. An attic above and a cellar below provided more space than a single couple could ever need.

A front porch completed the picture, with a bench ingeniously hung from the porch roof by chains, creating a swing for quiet nights or happy children.

Children had never happened, though. Try as they might, children never came. Eleanor sometimes wondered, in the late hours after midnight, whether it was worse to carry a child only to lose it or never manage to conceive at all. She was forced to conclude that they were both sadly pitiful, either way. Her husband was dead, and there wouldn't be any second chances, and all the Jessups could do was fill their empty house with grown people.

Starting with Eleanor. At least the grown people they seemed to take in needed them. That was important.

Lucas set her suitcase down with a heavy thump. All the bedrooms were on the second floor, and Eleanor's looked out over the front of the house. The walls were painted white, and blue calico curtains fluttered over the window.

"It's not much, but I hope you'll like it." Susannah surveyed the room with hands on her hips. There wasn't much furniture, only a bed, a wardrobe, and a wash-stand, and none of it was new. Still, it was more than Eleanor had had to herself in a long time.

"I love it. It's perfect for me," she said honestly. The idea of some real privacy for the first time in her life was delightful. Even when she'd been married, she'd never really had a room to herself.

Lucas left the room, and the two ladies busied them-selves unpacking Eleanor's trunk. Susannah hummed to herself as she carefully placed Eleanor's brush and comb on the wash stand. Eleanor herself hung up her few clothes in the wardrobe, feeling profoundly embar-rassed that this was all she had to bring. A few skirts, a couple of blouses, and two jackets were all the clothes she had in the world. All of her material possessions fit into a single suitcase with ease.

Her lack of clothes brought another pressing issue to mind.

"I know it's a bit late for me to be bringing this up now that I'm here," Eleanor said, blushing hotly, "but I can't really afford to pay for my lodgings. I used al-most every penny I had just to get here."

She twiddled her fingers awkwardly, avoiding Su-sannah's eye when she looked at her in surprise.

"You're our guest," Susannah said. "You don't have to pay for anything."

Eleanor shook her head.

"I can't impose on you like that, though." She looked

down at her hands and then back up to Susannah's sweet face. "If I have to pay my way in my own family's home, I certainly can't rely on your charity for the rest of my life."

Susannah's smile faded to a frown. She was silent for a moment.

"Well, you can help out around the house. I said in my letters that I needed a hand around here. You'll just have to dust your way into our good graces."

She was trying to joke, but Susannah really didn't find much humor in the situation. Eleanor was too beaten down to expect kindness, even from her own family. They'd gotten her out of Boston just in time.

Chapter Three

Over the next several days, Eleanor took over almost every chore in the house. She swept and scrubbed the floors, cooked the supper and washed the dishes, then took the laundry out to wash before Susannah could lift a finger. Finally, Susannah was forced to have a talk with her.

"Really, Eleanor, you're not my maid," she said seriously. "I'm not the sort to go having you do everything for me. We should at least take turns with the work, or else I'll grow so lazy you'll have to carry me to church."

Eleanor smiled. She actually had far less to do here than she had in Boston. A household of three could only produce so much work in comparison with one of eight, no matter what the size of the home itself.

"It's really no trouble. I don't know what I'd do with myself otherwise."

Susannah shook her head.

"I don't know what to do with myself, now. You're going to turn me into a lady of leisure, and then you'll leave one day, and where will that leave me?"

"If it bothers you that much, we can share the work.

Starting tomorrow." Eleanor disappeared into the kitchen before Susannah could say another word. She sighed and returned to the sitting room, plopping down into a seat. She picked up some needlework, but put it down again almost immediately.

Poor Eleanor. She was such a hard worker, and she never had anything come of it. Susannah could open her home and her heart to her, but there must be something more she could do. Eleanor deserved more.

Frowning, Susannah watched her slip past the open doorway with a broom in her hand. She must have been so lonely, too. She had lost her husband without even the comfort of a child to remember him by.

Suddenly, a smile lit up Susannah's face. She knew *exactly* what to do with Eleanor. And for the first step, she needed a new dress.

Chapter Four

The next day after breakfast, Susannah hitched up the buggy and dragged her guest into it for a ride to town. She had told Eleanor that they were running an errand, but refused to be more specific than that. She did, however, look extremely pleased with herself. When the buggy came to a stop in front of a dressmaker's shop, Eleanor stared with wide eyes.

"What are we doing here?" she asked nervously. Did Susannah think her clothes were too poor? She didn't have money for a new dress. Eleanor had spent almost everything she had on train tickets.

"A treat for you," Susannah said, smiling at her. "Every woman deserves a new dress every now and then. Come now, you probably haven't had a new dress in a year."

Eleanor hated to admit it, but it was true. She took immaculate care of her clothes because they had to last. She couldn't afford to replace them.

"I can't say you're wrong," she murmured.

"Of course you can't," Susannah said cheerfully. "Now let's have some fun."

The next hour was a whirlwind of fashion plates and fabric samples. Eleanor was shocked at how up-to-date the fashions in Colorado were. She'd thought someplace this far west would be behind the times, but the designs she was shown weren't that far off from what the ladies in Boston wore.

News travels quickly these days, she reflected. *After all, it only took me a few days to get here.*

In theory Eleanor picked patterns and fabrics, but really it was Susannah doing the picking. Without her friend lurking at her side making suggestions, Eleanor would have bought something very different.

Normally, Eleanor would have sewn her clothes herself, and would have made them as she could manage while still maintaining propriety. Under Susannah's guidance, Eleanor was measured up for a matching skirt and jacket, in pale blue stripes with just a tasteful bit of dark blue ribbon for trim. This was to be well tailored, as Susannah insisted that she stop trying to hide herself under a flour sack. She hadn't even seen the finished article, and Eleanor already felt self-conscious.

"A nice suit like that you can wear just about anywhere," Susannah said. "Out for walk, to church… We can get you a little bonnet, too. With a white feather in it." From the gleam in Susannah's eye, Eleanor rather suspected that Susannah was the one who wanted a bonnet with a white feather. "And stop making that face. You're a lovely young woman. Nobody is going to be offended if you wear clothes that actually fit."

Eleanor shifted uncomfortably. It was going to take her some time to get used to not hiding her body, probably longer than Susannah would like. Susannah would like her to be comfortable already. Eleanor would have liked to never get comfortable with it at all, but she was determined to be brave. *After all,* she thought, *I've already come this far.*

At Susannah's insistence, a couple of blouses were added to the pile, along with material to make another new skirt.

"You really don't have to do this for me," Eleanor said again as Susannah discussed payment with the shop assistant. "I can make do with what I have. You're already doing so much."

Susannah close her pocketbook with a definitive snap.

"Well, if you're that worried about it you can make us an extra special supper. I may have been here for a few years, but I still remember your cooking," Susannah said, smiling. Eleanor didn't think that was an equivalent exchange, but she quickly agreed.

"How about this Sunday?" Susannah suggested. "We can have a nice Sunday supper."

"Sounds perfect. I'd love to cook for you!"

Chapter Five

"I want to invite one of your friends over, to introduce to Eleanor," Susannah said that evening, after Eleanor had gone to bed. She and Lucas were together in the sitting room, watching the fire sink lower on the hearth.

"One of my single friends, I assume," Lucas said, looking at her from the corner of his eye.

"They might just happen to be single, yes. It might just happen that one of them falls in love with a friend of mine who also happens to be single."

"No. We're not doing that," Lucas said flatly. Susannah huffed.

"Lucas!"

"Susannah, I won't have you using my friends as a courting service. I have a reputation to maintain and professional relationships to uphold. None of that is compatible with also trying to marry people off to my wife's widowed friends."

"*You* don't have to try to marry anyone off," Susannah said innocently. "I'll handle that part all by myself. I think I'll be good at it, too."

"I said no and I meant no." Reaching over, he picked up a newspaper and opened it with an air of finality.

Susannah put her knitting aside and got up, sitting on the sofa next to Lucas.

"Don't you want what's best for Eleanor?" she said, leaning her head against his shoulder. Sighing, he laid the paper on his knees so he could put his arm around her shoulders, holding her tightly.

"Of course, I want what's best for Eleanor, but I also want what's best for my friends. Interfering in their personal lives isn't helping. I would advise you not to interfere too much with Eleanor, either. You may wind up hurting more than you help."

Lucas enforced his point with a gentle kiss to Susannah's forehead, but she continued to look unhappy.

"People need to find their own way in life. I'm sure Eleanor will find her path soon. And she'll be pleased with herself for figuring it all out on her own," he said. "Now, let's go to bed."

It seemed to Susannah, as she followed Lucas up the stairs, that finding your own path was all well and good, but one could probably find it much faster if someone else showed you the way.

Her determination to find a husband for Eleanor grew with each step she took. Eleanor's trip to Colorado was going to be a very fruitful one, indeed.

Chapter Six

Eleanor awoke Sunday morning feeling cheerful. It was going to be her first service in Rocky Ridge, Colorado, and she was eager to meet the pastor and all her fellow church-goers. If she was going to make any friends other than Susannah anywhere in this town, it would be there.

Not only that, her new suit had arrived the day before. It was wonderful, the light blue jacket tailored in such a way that Eleanor hardly recognized the woman in the Jessups' small mirror. Where Eleanor was dumpy, this woman had a well-shaped, if a bit large, figure. And Susannah had been right that that shade of blue was very flattering. Eleanor hadn't had something that nice to wear in years. It made her feel excited, like a young girl going to her first dance instead of a widow going to church.

The three of them all piled into the buggy after breakfast and rolled into town. They were far from alone. The churchyard was full of horses and carts, buggies and wagons, and a fair number of people simply walked. Right before they walked through the church door, Eleanor was struck by a wave of anxiety.

She was the new person in town. Surely everyone would be looking at her. And she was wearing that suit. Susannah said it looked wonderful, but Eleanor was sure all it did was make her look like a big, round, blue poof, despite what the mirror had shown her.

Being the local sheriff, Lucas took a seat near the front of the church, and it seemed like a torturously long walk. If it weren't for Susannah pulling her along by the arm, she might have fled.

Eleanor was right about being watched. Heads craned on necks as people tried to get a look at her, some more subtle than others. Susannah cast an eye over the crowd as they walked to the front pews, searching for any eligible bachelors who looked interested.

To her surprise, the man who came to mind was one who wasn't in the church at all. Matthew Connor, a successful rancher and close friend of Lucas's, rarely attended church. Susannah knew for a fact that he was extremely single. He hadn't done much other than build his ranch for ten years.

Matthew was a wealthy man, and a kind one. He would treat Eleanor well if they were to marry. Of that she couldn't be more certain.

Now she just had to figure out how to make them get married.

After the service ended and Eleanor had been introduced to Pastor Judd and what seemed like every lady in town, the Jessups and company left the church. Susannah looked down the road as Lucas untied the horses, bouncing on her feet with some inexplicable energy that he had long since stopped questioning.

"I'm going to run down and visit old Mrs. Henderson," she said suddenly, folding her bag behind her back. "She's been poorly, lately, you know. No need to wait, I can just walk home. Eleanor should probably go on back with you if you don't mind. She must be tired after meeting all these people, and I hardly need company just to visit Mrs. Henderson."

With that, she dashed off. Lucas gave her a suspicious look, but didn't argue. Susannah had already disappeared down the street, anyway. Hopping over wagon ruts, she crossed over to the Rocky Ridge branch of the Rocky Mountain Cattle Association and pushed open the door. Her face lit up as she stepped inside.

"Matthew Connor!" Susannah said, tripping lightly across the room. "Just the man I was hoping to see…"

Chapter Seven

"There's going to be a guest?" Eleanor said blankly. Susannah was standing in the kitchen door, looking extremely pleased with herself.

"Yes. I just so happened to run into a friend of Lucas's while I was at the store, and I invited him over for supper tonight."

Lucas, who was passing through the main hall on his way out back, stopped to butt in.

"Susannah…"

His wife glared at him.

"Don't give me that look. If it was up to you we'd never see anyone at all. We haven't seen Matthew in quite a while, and I'd love to see him for more than a quick hello on the street. And it's only proper we start introducing our guest to the town."

Lucas shook his head and rolled his eyes.

"Do as you wish, my love, but don't come running to me if it backfires." Leaning down, Lucas kissed the top of Susannah's head, and proceeded outside.

"What does he mean by that?" Eleanor asked, giving Susannah a look. Susannah just smiled, putting her hands on her hips.

"Never you mind. Now, what are we doing here?"

Chapter Eight

The supper guest, to Eleanor's consternation, turned out to be a very handsome man. He was tall and broad, with glinting steel-blue eyes and dark, somewhat unruly hair. A square jaw covered in dark stubble looked appealing rather than messy. To say Eleanor was intimidated was an understatement. She'd never been comfortable around handsome men, and the sight of Susannah winking at her just made it worse.

"Eleanor, this is Matthew Connor. He's an old friend of Lucas's. Matthew, this is Eleanor Trimble. She's an old friend of mine who was widowed recently. How nice for two of our oldest friends to meet!"

Matthew Connor politely dipped his head to Eleanor, whom Susannah had dragged out of the kitchen with her apron on for introductions.

"Now, supper's just about ready, so if you'll excuse us we'll go get everything set up." Susannah turned to the kitchen, allowing a grateful Eleanor to escape. She was already dreading this meal.

With Susannah's assistance, Eleanor brought all the dishes to the table and signaled to the gentlemen that everything was ready. Her hands almost shook as she took her apron off. What was Susannah thinking? Inviting a handsome man like that to eat with *her?* She could only imagine what he was going to think of a fat, dumpy woman who made pies.

Matthew Connor turned out to be a perfect gentleman, which from Eleanor's point of view only made things worse. Susannah had cheerfully introduced her as a widow, which had earned her a sympathetic look from Matthew. Now Eleanor was faced with a handsome man's pity for the duration of the meal.

Matthew himself was a rancher. He lived outside of town, in what was according to Susannah quite a large house, from which he managed herds of cattle. It was just about the most Western thing Eleanor had ever heard, and if she wasn't slightly terrified of him she would have asked if he spent his time on the range like a cowboy.

Silently, she spooned up her peas.

Matthew himself was rather puzzled. Eleanor seemed like a sweet enough woman, and she was certainly a good cook, but she hardly spoke during the meal. Even then, she only contributed to the conversation when directly spoken to. She refused to look up, either, keeping her eyes glued to her plate.

He didn't understand what she had to be so shy about. Eleanor wasn't just sweet, she was also quite pretty. Her figure may have been on the large side, but it was still a pleasing shape, and it gave her cheeks a certain plumpness that was quite charming. Her eyes were also beautiful, when he actually got a look at them. They were a deep, warm shade of brown, like a good cup of coffee, and her eyelashes were thick and dark. Even her hair was lovely, twisted up into a thick, glossy brown knot behind her head.

No, Matthew didn't understand what she was shy about at all.

"Isn't this chicken just lovely, Lucas? I must admit, I missed Eleanor's cooking since I came to Colorado." Susannah gave a Matthew a meaningful look, and Lucas rolled his eyes.

Well, that probably wasn't helping. Matthew got the feeling that if he was going to get to know Eleanor at all, he was going to have to get her away from Susannah.

The opportunity to do that came sooner than he would have expected, and from Susannah herself. The crowning glory of the meal was a rhubarb pie, made with last year's preserves, with a perfectly flaky crust worked into decorative ridges. Susannah took over the duty of cutting everyone a large slice.

"It's such a lovely afternoon," she said, handing a piece to Matthew. "Why don't the two of you eat this on the porch swing? It's always good to take in some fresh air."

"But…" Before Eleanor could voice her complaint, Susannah thrust a plate of pie into her hands and pushed her toward the door. "Susannah, I don't—"

"I would enjoy that, if it's all right with you, ma'am," Matthew said. His voice was quiet but deep, easy to hear despite its low tone. Eleanor hesitated, then nodded. If Susannah was determined to make her embarrass herself in front of this man, she might as well get it over with now.

Matthew quietly led the way to the front porch, opening the door for her to pass. As they sat down on the swing, Eleanor realized he was even wider than she was. Between the two of them, they spanned almost the entire bench. She could tell by looking at him, though, that there was nothing soft or doughy about him. That was the body of a man who worked hard, every day.

They sat in silence for a short while, just eating their pie. Eleanor had expected silence. She certainly didn't have anything to say to a handsome rancher. To her surprise, though, the silence was pleasant. Matthew was a large man, but not an imposing one, and now that she didn't have to look directly at his face Eleanor actually felt quite comfortable. If all they did was sit and eat pie, she could handle this quite well.

Matthew cleared her throat, turning slightly to look at her.

"So what brings you to our fair city of Rocky Ridge?" he asked, sliding his fork through the pie.

Eleanor hesitated before answering. She could tell him something vague and evasive, but something about the warmth in his eyes made her want to be honest.

"I needed to get away from Boston," she said, her voice cautious. "My life pretty much fell apart. I got married three years ago, to a shopkeeper named John Trimble. We conceived right away." She blushed at this personal admission to a total stranger. She shook her head almost involuntarily.

Matthew nodded for her to continue, interested to hear her story.

"Um, then I lost the baby. Three months after that, John got influenza and died. I went back home to my parents, but my father lost his job and the rest of us couldn't make up for his lost salary. Money was really scarce."

"That's more misfortune than most could handle. I'm sorry you've had that fall at your doorstep." Matthew gave her a concerned look, but there was no pity.

"Everyone has misfortune. Some, more than others, I suppose. But, anyway, I sold pies and baked goods in the market every day of the week, but it wasn't enough to make ends meet. All I got was resentment for being another mouth to feed in the house. When Susannah suggested I come out here to visit her, I didn't have a reason not to come."

Matthew stared at her for a moment, and Eleanor held her breath, waiting for his complete reaction. Surely now he'd think she was being pathetic, like most of the population of Boston.

To her surprise, his expression was compassionate.

"That's an awful lot of trouble for an awfully short life," he said, looking down at the boards of the porch.

"I suppose it is. But as I said, most people meet hardship at least once in a lifetime," Eleanor said.

There was a long pause, each of them lost in their own thoughts.

"My pa moved us all out to Colorado when I was just a young'n," Matthew said suddenly. "He wanted to prospect for gold, but he didn't have the heart to leave us all behind. The family didn't have much back in Ohio, and he wanted to give us all a better life."

Eleanor watched him speak. Matthew's face was serious, almost hard.

"Less than a year after we got here, he was lost in a blizzard and got the pneumonia. He didn't survive, either. Ever since then I've been determined to do what he couldn't, and make a good life for us out here. My Ma and my sisters all live off my ranch, and I'm only going to make it bigger and better."

It was Eleanor's turn to look at the porch. That kind of determination seemed amazing to her. Life had kicked her to the ground and all she wanted to do was give up. Matthew Connor had rolled with the punches and built a kingdom.

After a moment, Matthew cleared his throat.

"I'm terribly sorry, ma'am," he said, blushing faintly under his dark stubble. "This is awful dour conversation for a beautiful lady like you the first time we ever even talk."

Eleanor blushed and shook her head.

"I'm the one who started it," she said. "Life gives us all difficulties, I suppose."

"That it does," Matthew agreed.

The conversation lasted long after the pair ran out of pie. They talked of everything under the sun; what books they'd read and which ones they liked, places they'd been and where they wanted to go. Matthew told Eleanor about long nights on the range, keeping watch over cattle to stop rustlers and coyotes, and Eleanor described seeing the ships come and go in the Boston Harbor.

"I've never seen the ocean," Matthew confessed. The pair were now gently rocking back and forth on the porch swing, sitting at either end in complete ease. "I'd like to someday, but I don't know when the cattle business is likely to take me there."

"Well, I'd never seen a mountain until a few days ago." Eleanor smiled as she remembered her journey across the country. "The train passed through the Appalachians, but those are like a wrinkled sheet compared to these mountains. The country here is more beautiful than I ever could have imagined."

"It's wonderful here in the fall," Matthew said, his gruff voice surprisingly intimate. "The aspen trees all turn yellow and it looks like the hills are covered in gold."

"That sounds simply lovely," Eleanor said. Her tone was just as soft as his. "I'd love to see it, but I don't know if I'll be here that long."

Matthew was silent for a moment, staring into the distance.

"Would you like to have supper with me next Sunday, Miss Eleanor?" he said abruptly. Eleanor turned to him in surprise.

"I… Well, I suppose so."

Matt nodded.

"If that's settled, I'd best be going, then." He rose to his feet. Eleanor stood, too, twisting her fingers like a schoolgirl. "I'll see you next Sunday."

Eleanor just nodded silently, and Matthew headed for the stable. Quietly, Eleanor stepped inside the house to find Susannah hiding behind the front window, looking like a child caught with her hand in the cookie jar.

"What are you doing?" Eleanor asked, crossing her arms.

"I'm just looking out for your best interests," Susannah said earnestly.

Lucas, who was sitting by the fire with a newspaper, shook his head.

"I appreciate the thought, but all the same I'd prefer it if you not spy on me," Eleanor said.

"I'll promise with my hand on the Bible," Susannah declared, and Eleanor rolled her eyes. Susannah had always been theatrical.

"That's not necessary. Just don't peep at me between the curtains."

"I most certainly won't."

"You do realize she's just going to find another way to watch you, right?" Lucas said, glancing up from his paper. Susannah made a sour face at him.

"Come, husband. You're supposed to assist me in life's endeavors."

Lucas gave her a dry stare. "I thought man wasn't meant to work on the Sabbath."

"But you forget, I'm a woman," Susannah replied evenly.

"Oh, I remember. I've long given up trying to fathom your ways."

Eleanor watched the couple banter back and forth with a twinge of envy. Even when John had been alive, they'd never truly joked around like that. She had to wonder if life had that much harmony in store for her, or if she'd remain a widow forever.

She had a good feeling about Matthew Connor. She hoped she wouldn't come to regret it.

Chapter Nine

Thursday arrived, and Eleanor hadn't yet begun to regret agreeing to see Matthew. She was actually quite looking forward to it, humming happily as she walked to town with her basket. Susannah had sent her off to the store to buy writing paper while she sorted through freshly picked early spring vegetables to prepare them for pickling.

Eleanor had grown familiar with the route to town over the week. It was quite straightforward once you know which branch you were supposed to turn down. She walked at a leisurely pace, and soon she reached the spot where all the smaller paths joined together. As she passed on to the main road, someone called her name.

It was the subject of her thoughts, Matthew Connor. He was riding down the middle path, on a large bay horse, and he brought the animal to a stop as he reached where she stood.

"Good afternoon, ma'am." He tipped his hat, nodding politely. "What brings you out here all alone this time of day?"

"I'm going to the dry goods store. An errand for Su-sannah," Eleanor replied. Without her noticing, she held her basket behind her back, like an embarrassed girl. Matthew swung down off his horse.

"If that's the case, I'll walk with you," he said. "If that's all right with you, ma'am, of course."

"Call me Ellie," Eleanor said, feeling very bold. "That's what all my friends call me."

Matthew nodded, not smiling much, but she could tell he was happy.

"Call me Matt, then."

"Won't your horse get bored?" She glanced back at his horse with a raise of her eyebrow. The animal was following them sedately, Matthew leading it along by the reins as they walked. He gave her a blank look, then laughed.

"He probably thinks he's lucky." He stopped briefly to rub the horse's nose affectionately. "Not have to carry a heavy old codger like me around town, for once."

They continued to walk in companionable silence.

"Were you still planning on coming to supper on Sunday, ma—I mean, Ellie?"

"Well, yes, I was planning on it," Eleanor said. She could feel herself blushing slightly.

"Well, if that's the case I'll come around in my buggy after church and take you to my place," he said.

Eleanor nodded her agreement to the plan. "Do you cook? Everyone says cowboys don't eat anything but beans," she asked.

That prompted another laugh from Matthew. "That's not too far off, to tell the truth. A lot of beans. Bacon. Coffee. Canned fruit, if you're lucky. Potatoes, sometimes. And beef, of course. There was also bread, but we didn't have a cook most of the time, and it came out burnt more often than it came out edible."

Eleanor smiled and chuckled lowly. "Burned bread doesn't sound like a good thing at all."

Matthew shook his head. "Nothing makes you appreciate a good cook like living off salt pork and beans six months out of the year. I miss the range sometimes, but I'll never miss range food."

"It must be lonely, for the wives left behind," Eleanor said quietly.

"Not a lot of cowboys are married," Matthew said. "Most of 'em are pretty young men. It's a hard job. Do it for long enough and it breaks you down. No, most men want to be a little more stable than that before they take a wife."

"I see." Eleanor felt a little silly at the discussion about husbands and wives. She didn't want him to think she was hinting at anything. Susannah already did enough hinting for the both of them. She took a deep breath. "Well, if you ever need bread, I can promise you not to burn it."

"I'm sure you wouldn't," Matthew said, smiling. Then he asked about her baking, and a conversation about how many kinds of pies she knew how to make started that lasted until they reached the store.

"I'm afraid we'll have to discuss the intricacies of chicken pies later," he said, nodding toward the storefront. Eleanor was surprised. She'd been so busy talking she hadn't even noticed how far they'd come.

"Oh, I see. Well, thank you for walking with me. I suppose I'll see you Sunday?"

"I suppose you will. I'll see you then, Miss Ellie."
Matthew tipped his hat again and swung on to his horse,
trotting away down the road.

Chapter Ten

Eleanor happily stepped into the mercantile, almost floating on the tips of her toes. She couldn't remember the last time she'd had such an engaging conversation. She didn't think she'd ever had one with a man. Eleanor was nearly starting to be happy that Susannah kept dropping such heavy matrimonial hints.

The store wasn't terribly busy, a few men and one woman standing around examining the goods. Eleanor went straight to the counter, making her request. The store kept its paper in the back, where it couldn't be dirtied, and the clerk gave Eleanor the sample book showing what types they had. While she flipped through the pages, a lady entered the shop, carrying a large basket.

Everyone in the room jumped as the woman who'd already been there squealed loudly. She rushed over to the newcomer, peering into her basket.

"Oh, she's out and about, now!" she said. "Are you sure it's all right? She's still so small."

Ah. Eleanor thought. *A baby.*

"It's all right. She's well tucked up, and she's got that

little cap my mother made. She's got fifteen caps, actually. Mama got a little…let's say enthusiastic."

Eleanor flipped through the paper samples again, refusing to look over at the chattering pair. It had been some time since she'd lost her baby, but it still hurt sometimes to see other happy mothers. She didn't want to stir up those thoughts, again, even though she hoped to have a family one day.

Though her spirits were low now, deep inside she wanted the chance to be a wife and mother. She just had no idea how she'd get there. Staying positive and looking forward with hope was a challenge, but she was heartened that possibly her time in Rocky Ridge would help her not-so-sunny outlook.

"Fifty sheets of this one, please," she said, pointing to a plain, white sheet of letter paper. The clerk nodded, and disappeared into the back room.

"Your mother always did want a granddaughter," the squealer said. "I hope she doesn't make your boys jealous, spoiling that child."

"They're already jealous," the young mother shook her head. "You know how Jesse is."

Eleanor sighed, feeling her spirits sag again. Some people had all the good fortune in life. The clerk returned with her paper and she paid, tucking the bundle into her basket for the walk home. The two friends and the baby were standing in front of the door, and there was no way Eleanor could avoid getting a tiny glimpse.

She was a perfect little girl, with fat pink cheeks and chubby little hands, tucked in a soft blanket with a little pink cap on her bald head. The mother reached down to stroke her cheek as Eleanor passed. It was almost more than she could stand, seeing that tiny, perfect little baby. Quickly, she dashed out the door and onto the busy street.

Eleanor wiped her eyes as she began the long walk home. She didn't usually get upset like that, but she'd been taken by surprise. Her conversation with Matt had left her so unguarded that the feelings of loss and sadness had washed right over her.

Matthew. Matt...

What was she thinking? Laughing and talking about pies with a man, after so many people had died? If there was any justice in the world, Eleanor would be back in Boston, living with John and their son. Not standing in a corner store in Colorado, envying other women's babies.

Taking a deep breath, Eleanor blew her nose and tried to take command of herself. She had to stop being so silly, letting her emotions get the better of her like that. Even the happy ones. She had no business being so happy with another man, when her baby and husband lay buried half a country away.

Happy. Eleanor was surprised as she thought the word. Yes, she had been happy. Talking with Matthew over the last few days had made her very happy. It was such a strange sensation, to be feeling something other than sadness again. Eleanor wasn't sure she liked it. It would be much better to just go on feeling nothing, and respect the memory of her loved ones.

Filled with determination, Eleanor hurried home.

Chapter Eleven

"What do you mean you don't want to go?" Susannah stood with her hands on her hips, giving Eleanor a demanding look. "You were perfectly happy to go just the other day!"

"Now, Susannah, don't push her," Lucas said. They had just returned from church that Sunday, and he was taking off his good coat to put it away. Eleanor herself was standing behind an armchair, as though she were using it as a shield.

"But you were looking forward to it so much," Susannah said. "Matt was, too. I know for a fact he's been worrying about what to feed you."

"I just don't feel like it's proper," Eleanor said, shifting uncomfortably under Susannah's scrutiny.

"It's not proper to answer an ad in the paper from a strange man, either, but that worked out well for me."

Lucas made a face at his wife.

"Susannah, I'm not you. It's not proper for me. I'm a widow. John hasn't even been dead two years," Eleanor said desperately.

Susannah opened her mouth, ready to argue back

when Lucas put a hand on her shoulder. She sighed, looking exasperated.

"All right. But I want you to attend just this one supper. It wouldn't be right to make him go to all that trouble and then refuse to go."

Eleanor didn't like it, but she couldn't deny that it would be horrible of her to do that to Matt, and unfair of her to not give him any explanation. She would just have to go to the supper and make it clear she wasn't interested.

What a lovely afternoon to look forward to. She groaned inwardly and tried to get her mind focused on what had to be done.

Chapter Twelve

Matthew showed up at one o'clock on the dot, and Eleanor waved goodbye to Susannah and Lucas. Matthew stepped down to help her into the gig before taking up the reins.

"Good afternoon," he said, glancing sideways at her. "I hope your Sunday has been pleasant so far. Church was uplifting, I imagine?"

"Quite inspirational, thank you," Eleanor replied stiffly. She could just see Matthew frown in puzzlement from the corner of her eye.

"You sure?" he asked.

"I'm quite sure, Mr. Connor."

At that, Matthew turned his head sharply to look at her. Eleanor just bit her lip, folding her hands in her lap. The ride to the ranch was long, made longer by their lack of conversation. Matthew made a few attempts at conversation, but didn't get more than a few words in response.

Finally, they arrived at a long, open field, where a large wooden building sat surrounded by smaller outbuildings. The design was simple, but the structures were well built. Care had obviously gone into their construction. As they grew closer, Eleanor could see the details of the main building. A rag rug for people to wipe their boots on, bunches of herbs and garlic hanging to dry from the porch eaves, an old horseshoe nailed up over the door. Little touches of warmth that made the otherwise stark building homey and inviting.

Matthew pulled the horse to a stop and hopped down to help Eleanor to the ground.

"My house." He gestured to the house in front of them. "It's not two floors like the Jessup's, but we've got plenty of room. All the hired hands stay in these buildings round back. There's a kitchen garden, as well." Matthew looked at Eleanor, as if he were slightly anxious that she wouldn't approve.

"It's lovely," she said honestly, with more admiration in her voice that she intended. "The view out over this field is wonderful."

Matthew smiled.

"It is," he agreed, putting a hand on her arm. "May I show you inside?"

Eleanor chided herself as they entered the house. She had to be more careful about how she acted.

The inside of the house was even warmer and more welcoming than the outside. The walls were papered in cream paper, with little sprigs of flowers scattered across it. Homemade samplers hung on the walls along with the occasional photograph.

There was also an older woman in the entry hall, wearing a plain but fine shirtwaist and skirt. Looking at her, Eleanor realized she must be Matthew's mother.

"Miss Eleanor?" she asked, smiling. "I'm Mrs. Connor. It's lovely to meet you."

Eleanor shook her hand, more than a little uncomfortable. Just what had Matthew told her? That they were already engaged?

"Wonderful to meet you, too," she said woodenly.

"I'm afraid my daughters are all out of the house at the moment," Mrs. Connor said. "My youngest is off helping the oldest with her children. She married and lives in Colorado Springs, now."

"That's too bad," Eleanor said. "Um, that they're away, not that she got married." She flushed deeply as she quickly corrected herself.

Mrs. Connor laughed and waved her arm.

"Well, aren't you charming, indeed." Coming from anyone else Eleanor would have suspected sarcasm, but the older woman seemed too genuinely amiable for that. "Come along now, into the dining room. We've got everything ready."

Putting her hand on Eleanor's arm, she pulled her along the hall to a comfortably furnished dining room. The table was already spread out, with three place settings and dishes filled with spring vegetables and roast beef, all set on a pristine white table cloth.

"I'm afraid I can't return the favor of cooking your supper myself," Matt said, pulling out the chair for Eleanor to sit down. "I'm not so sure you'd like my cowboy cooking. I always burn the bread."

"I can second that," Mrs. Connor said, making a face. "Matt had to cook for me once when I was ill. I think it might have made me worse."

Eleanor laughed, but the smile quickly faded from her lips. What was she doing here, laughing with the mother of a man she had no intention of marrying? Coming here had been a mistake, no matter what Susannah said about it.

The meal was delicious, but the conversation dragged the mood down. More accurately, the lack of conversation dragged it down. Mrs. Connor made a valiant attempt at keeping things going, asking Eleanor questions and remarking on her answers, but it was difficult to get her to say anything more than a few words at a time.

By the time dessert rolled around, things had sunk into silence. Eleanor ate her cake quickly, barely noting its taste. She just wanted the visit to finish as quickly as possible. Thanking a puzzled and concerned Mrs. Connor for the meal, Eleanor practically ran out to the front porch.

Once out of the house she took a deep breath. *Well, that could have gone worse, I suppose,* Eleanor thought. There was the quiet sound of footsteps, and Matthew came out onto the porch. He stood there in silence for a moment, watching her with the same puzzled concern his mother had had.

"I was thinking that after we ate, I could show you around the ranch," he said. "Since you've been so curious about how we run things out here."

"I'd rather not," Eleanor said quietly, looking at the floor of the porch.

Matthew gave her a piercing look, then sighed. "All right, I'll ask. Ellie, what's wrong?"

"Nothing's wrong. I just don't want to tour the ranch."

Matthew turned to face her head on, crossing his arms. "Why did you come to this supper?"

"I wanted to tell you," Eleanor said quickly, spitting the words out before she could lose her determination, "that I don't think we should keep seeing each other."

Matt stared at her, his face expressionless.

"My husband hasn't even been dead for very long.

It's not right for me to be seeing a man like this so soon. At least not quite yet. And I've only gotten into town. I probably won't be staying here forever."

He continued to stare in silence, and Eleanor looked down at the porch, too embarrassed and miserable to look at him.

"I assumed you were nervous," Matt said, his voice a little gruff. "You were quiet as a mouse, last week. You might have just had an attack of nerves, again. Forgive me for being blunt, but Ellie, you're smarter than this."

Eleanor looked up at him in shock. What was that supposed to mean?

"I know you must have loved your husband dearly, and your baby, too. But they've been dead for more than two years. That's what you told me. Sitting at home moping isn't going to make them come back."

Moping? That's what her mother had always said. That she did nothing but mope. Now Eleanor was getting angry.

"At some point you're going to have to start your life again, or else you'll waste away." Matthew reached out and took one of her trembling hands. "Let me help you. You don't have to be alone for the rest of your life."

Eleanor yanked her hand away from his.

"I'm sorry, Mr. Connor, but I'm sure you don't need a fat, pathetic wife moping around your ranch. You can do a great deal better than me. Now if you don't mind, I'd like to go home… I mean back to the Jessup place."

Matthew watched her in silence for a long moment, then sighed.

"As you wish," he said quietly. "It's too far to walk, so I'll drive you back."

Eleanor almost refused the offer, but he was right. It

would have been a long, lonely walk from his ranch house to the Jessups'. She stood on the porch in silence while Matthew fetched his horse and hitched it up to the gig.

"After you." He held out a hand to help her up, and Eleanor gritted her teeth. She'd said such rude things to him, and he still acted like a gentlemen. She really didn't deserve to spend her life with a man as good as that.

Staring miserably at the horse's back, Eleanor waited out the lonely, silent ride home. Susannah frowned when they arrived, both parties looking rather glum, but she kept her mouth shut. Lucas didn't look happy, either, and he stepped outside to speak to Matthew as Eleanor fled into the house.

"Ellie, are you all right?" Susannah asked softly. She'd followed Eleanor up to her room, where she had flopped face down on the bed.

"He said I'm stupid and pathetic," she mumbled into her pillow.

Susannah blinked. "Hmm. I really doubt he said that," she responded slowly. "You know you tend to see the worst in everything—at least right now. Matthew would never have said something that mean."

Eleanor rolled over, folding her hands over her stomach.

"Well, it doesn't matter, anyway. I already told him I don't want to see him anymore."

"Oh, Ellie. Give him another chance. Give yourself another chance," Susannah said. "You never know, he could be the one who finally makes you happy."

Little did Susannah know that that was actually the problem.

Chapter Thirteen

Matthew sat in his office the next Sunday morning, more disgruntled than he'd been in years. Eleanor still refused to talk to him. He'd gone to the Jessups' house twice that week, and both times Eleanor had run right up the stairs into her room. It was frustrating, to say the least.

If it was anyone other than Ellie, he would have given them up as a lost cause. He couldn't just leave a sweet woman like her to drown in misery. Too many things had happened to her already. Matthew knew she could have a happy life if she'd give herself the chance to live it, and he was determined to stick around and make her.

Matthew glanced at his clock. It was early yet, hardly nine o'clock. Eleanor and the Jessups would be going to church soon. He briefly thought of going, just for the chance of seeing her. She wouldn't be able to run away from him in a public space. Probably. She'd definitely know he'd gone there to see her.

Leaning back in his leather chair, Matthew put his feet up on the desk. Of course, it was a free country, and he was a free man. He could go to whatever church he wanted to in the whole state of Colorado. What's to say he didn't suddenly take it in his head to go to church? If it just happened to be the same church where Eleanor was, well, that was just a remarkable coincidence.

Matt decisively swung his feet to the floor and stood up. Grabbing his hat and coat, he was out the door in moments.

Chapter Fourteen

Eleanor was surprised to see Matt walk through the church door. He'd never attended since she'd been there, and she'd figured out that he wasn't particularly religious. She tried not to think about what his reasons for starting to care for church services now might be. Maybe he was just finally returning to the fold.

Pastor Judd stepped up to the pulpit, and the room grew quiet.

"This morning I wish to speak on a subject important to all of us, throughout our lives," he said, looking over his congregation. "The importance of marriage and love between husband and wife, and of love and charity in the rest of our lives."

Eleanor contained a groan. Pastor Judd must be doing this on purpose. Had Susannah gotten to him, too?

"The Bible has a great deal to say on the subject of husband and wife, and the roles each are to take in the family, but today I wish to focus on the importance of love. Without love, the marriage contract is only half fulfilled."

Pastor Judd looked around the room as he paused.

His eyes landed briefly on Eleanor and moved on to someone else.

"Men of all walks of life frequently speak of the benefits of marriage. A woman gains financial support and protection, while a man gains a helper in his life's labors, and someone to care for his home and children."

The pastor paused again, giving the crowd another penetrating stare. Thankfully, his watchful gaze skipped over Eleanor this time.

"I believe, however, that one of the most important benefits gained from marriage is the emotional and spiritual support gained from a bond based on mutual respect and affection. Together, a husband and wife are stronger. Together, they can struggle through disasters and losses, tragedies that might destroy one man alone."

He looked down at the pulpit where he turned a page in his Bible.

"The Bible itself admonishes a man to love his wife. Ephesians 5:25 says, *Husbands, love your wives, even as Christ also loved the church, and gave himself for it.* Man is meant to dedicate himself to the care of his wife and family, just as a woman is meant to support her husband. A heart filled with love and respect makes it a joy to care and provide for your partner, and to raise your children together into young men and women who will go on to marry other young men and women."

Looking up from his Bible, he smiled crookedly as his eyes made another sweep across the congregation.

"This is not to say that love is easy. Love may take a long time grow. A marriage may be started without love, but it should never be entered into without respect. Mutual respect between husband and wife will inevitably grow into love over time. It is impossible for people who live and struggle together to not grow to love each other, as God intended. Just as God loves his children on Earth, his desire is for us to love each other."

A few head nods from women and men in the congregation and a bit of noise from the Amen Corner allowed him to continue.

"Marriage is not the only relationship requiring us to show our love. Striving to love a stranger is complicated. Difficult even. But even the most distant of strangers deserves our compassion…"

Pastor Judd spoke on, but Eleanor was thinking about his words on marriage. It was as though the preacher had set out to pierce her in the heart, reminding her of everything she'd lost and what she could never have again. It was all very well to talk of love between husband and wife, until your husband died.

Her stomach gave an unpleasant lurch as she remembered that Matthew was listening to the same sermon. What in the world was he thinking, right now? Just last week she'd told him she had no intention of marrying him. A new twinge of guilt rose up in the depths of Eleanor's mind. She had denied Matthew the happiness of married life, too, just by refusing his offer.

Still, Eleanor hurriedly reasoned, *he's never actually been married. He can go on to marry whomever he pleases. He couldn't have had that much affection for* me. *He hardly knows me.*

The sermon went on while Eleanor was lost in her thoughts. Before she knew it, everyone was standing up, chatting and preparing to head home to their Sunday suppers. As they all filed toward the door, and from the corner of her eye Eleanor saw Matthew closing in.

There was no place to escape to, so she accepted her fate and waited.

Chapter Fifteen

She braced herself, expecting him to say something angry and resentful. But he just nodded his head and smiled.

"How are you this morning, Ellie?"

Eleanor pursed her lips. He still insisted on calling her that.

"Very well, Mr. Connor," she replied. After that her mouth was closed. If anyone was going to say anything, Matthew was going to do it.

"And how have things been going on the ranch?"

Or Susannah. She was happy to talk, too.

"Pretty well. The main herd's going to be calving over the next weeks. After that's over, I'm going to have to go out of town."

Can't come soon enough, Eleanor thought.

"Going to buy new stock?" Lucas asked.

"Thinking about it. Got the space and the resources to support more animals," Matthew said evenly.

Once the whole group had passed through the door, he made to leave them.

"I'll be seeing you around, Miss Ellie," he said, tipping his hat even as he put it on his head. Eleanor pointedly ignored him. Untying his horse, Matthew swung into the saddle and trotted away.

"Really, Ellie, you could have at least said goodbye," Susannah said, putting her hands on her hips.

"I don't want him to get the wrong idea," Eleanor said.

"Yes, we wouldn't want him thinking you're civil," Lucas said. Susannah scowled at him, but quietly noticed that he'd become just a little bit interested in how this went between Eleanor and Matthew.

"Just be nice." Susannah turned back to Eleanor. "I don't want to see you become bitter."

"I'm not bitter," Eleanor said firmly. *Just realistic.*

Lucas brought the buggy round and the trio drove home, Susannah busily scheming the entire way. She was already concocting a dozen plans to get Matthew and Eleanor in the same place.

Chapter Sixteen

A week later, soon after Matthew had returned from his business trip, Susannah dragged Eleanor into the back garden and gave her a hoe.

"We're expanding the garden," she said. "More room for quick-growing crops."

The kitchen garden wasn't large, and most of the space had been dedicated to crops with a long growing time, like melons and winter squash. It made sense that Susannah would want to expand. Still, cutting up underbrush wasn't Eleanor's favorite way to spend a morning.

The space for the expansion was already free of trees and bushes, but it was full of tall, waving grasses. Susannah and Eleanor had to clear the grass away before they could begin to turn the soil. It was hard, sweaty work, and it took the entire morning for them to clear the forty-foot-long patch and pile the grass to the side. Eleanor wiped her face with a handkerchief, already dreading the process of breaking up the soil.

While Eleanor was dreading the hours of backbreaking work it would take to break the soil, there was the rattle of a wagon out front.

"Right on time," Susannah said, wiping the sweat off her hands. Running to the side of the house, she shouted, "Come on round back!"

To Eleanor's dismay, Matthew Connor drove a small cart past the house. A small metal plow lay in the back.

"Matthew loaned us his plow last year to cut up the first garden," Susannah explained as Matthew hopped to the ground. "I just asked him to help out this time, since Lucas is so busy just now."

Eleanor sincerely doubted that was her only motivation, but she was too worn out by the morning's work to argue. Matthew unhitched the horse from the wagon, leading it over to stand by the cleared space.

"Good afternoon, Miss Ellie. Hold this." Grabbing Eleanor's hand, he put it on the horse's halter for her to hold it in place. Eleanor huffed indignantly, watching as he effortlessly pulled the heavy metal plow from the back of the wagon.

"We could do it by hand, but this way we can do it all in one day," Susannah said, coming to stand next to Eleanor. "It's much more convenient, and we'll actually get some planting done sooner rather than later."

"Very convenient, I'm sure," Eleanor murmured. Oh, yes, Susannah must have found this arrangement *very* convenient. For a lot of things.

Matthew set the plow down behind the horse and began hitching it up. Before long, he and his horse were making careful progress up the garden patch, leaving strips of turned sod behind them. Susannah watched for a few minutes, then clapped her hands.

"Well, I'll just go and make us up some lunch. You stay here, in case Matt needs any help." With that, she disappeared into the house. Eleanor sighed. Oh, yes. Very convenient, indeed.

Leaning against the tree in silence, she watched Matthew work. By the time Susannah returned with sandwiches and water, he'd already plowed a quarter of the garden. They all paused for a short meal, during which Susannah chattered cheerfully and Eleanor said nothing at all, and Matthew resumed work. Susannah quickly disappeared, finding some other excuse to leave him and Eleanor alone.

She set about cleaning up the house while the other two were out back, taking up the broom to sweep the floors. Susannah was just brushing the dust out the front door when Lucas rode up.

"Who's wagon is that?" he asked, frowning at the side of the house.

"Matt's. We started the garden today, and I asked him over to do the plowing," Susannah replied. Lucas raised an eyebrow at her.

"Since when do I not have time to plow my own garden?"

"Since Ellie and Matt needed to spend time alone together."

Lucas sighed and shook his head side to side. "Be careful, my love."

"Pish posh," Susannah said, flippantly dismissing his concern. "Matt wants to see her, too. He truly likes her. It's two against one, now. If you'd join in the process it would be three against one."

"I'm not sure I'm needed in the least. Poor Ellie. I wonder if she knows what she's up against." Shaking his head, Lucas headed into the house for lunch.

Chapter Seventeen

Matthew continued to appear at the Jessup household on a regular basis, helping to hoe or plant seeds, or even get down on hands and knees and weed. Eleanor was almost getting used to his presence, even though she still felt a prickle of annoyance at Susannah every time she heard his horse approaching.

She also felt a tiny bit of annoyance when Susannah invariably disappeared for the duration of his visit, leaving Eleanor alone with him. He would talk while they worked, speaking of what calves had been born and what cows were stubbornly holding out, all in a cheerful tone as though he didn't care whether Eleanor responded or not.

At first, she didn't. A few days after he'd told a particularly harrowing story about a weak calf, Eleanor asked how it was doing. The next visit, she admitted she'd never actually seen a newborn calf before, though she refused Matthew's invitation to come and look at them.

Over time he coaxed her to say more on her own. Gradually, she began to tell him about what she and Susannah had been doing around the house, or the quilt she had begun sewing blocks for, or how one of the hens had hidden her nest and now had a whole flock of chicks.

It wasn't much, but it was a start.

Eleanor and Matthew met every week at church as well, though Pastor Judd kindly refrained from making any more sermons about the benefits of married life. Matthew had originally come only to see Eleanor, but more and more he found himself appreciating the pastor's words. He even brought his mother, sometimes, and they went to sit with the Jessups, near the front of the church. They made polite conversation before and after the sermon, and Susannah cheerfully invited the both of them along for supper.

"You don't mind, do you, Eleanor?" she asked, turning to her with a wide smile. Eleanor shifted a little uncomfortably, but didn't refuse.

After that, it was a natural step for Matthew to start walking her home from church. His mother wasn't fond of coming to town and didn't always attend services, so when Matthew wasn't needed to drive her home he accompanied Eleanor instead. They would walk slowly, talking over the day's lessons. No matter how leisurely their pace, they always reached the house too fast. Eleanor even found herself looking forward to the next Sunday, when Matthew could walk her home again.

One hot, sunny Wednesday afternoon found Matthew at the Jessups', once again doing yard work with Eleanor. The pair knelt in the garden, pulling weeds from between the thriving potato plants.

"I think I know what you're thinking," Matthew said, glancing up at Eleanor.

"Do you?" Eleanor didn't even try to be cold to him

anymore. She couldn't bring herself to do it, settling for friendly yet non-committal.

"Yep. You feel guilty, don't you?"

Eleanor stopped and sat back on her heels, staring at him. Matthew continued weeding, unperturbed by her scrutiny.

"Just what is that supposed to mean?" Eleanor asked. Matthew took a deep breath before responding.

"When my pa died, my ma was beat down by it for a long time. I don't think she got over it for years, not until after I'd gotten the ranch going."

Eleanor watching him speak, the weeds forgotten.

"Right after I built the ranch house and got it all fitted up for her and my sisters, I found Ma sitting in her room just crying her eyes out. It took me a while to figure the problem, but I think I got it in the end."

Matthew stopped his own weeding, looking directly at Eleanor.

"She was feeling guilty. Guilty that she was living this comfortable life, while her husband was dead. He'd wanted a good life, and now here she was, living it without him. It was like betraying his memory, she thought, to be so happy when he couldn't be anything anymore."

Eleanor found herself unable to meet his gaze, and she turned her eyes down to the garden soil. Matthew took another deep breath.

"I told her," he said slowly, "that if Pa loved her at all, he wouldn't have wanted her to be sitting in a dark room crying twenty years after he'd gone. He'd still want her to be happy, and have a comfortable life. More than comfortable, if he had his way.

"The way I see it, it was more disrespectful to his

memory for her to not live her life. He brought us out west in the first place for her to have one."

Eleanor narrowed her eyes, but kept listening.

"It took her some time to think it through, but once she took the time to reconcile it all, she started feeling better. I know your husband's only been gone two years instead of twenty, but maybe it could help you to think of it that way, too."

Eleanor was silent when he finished speaking. Matthew watched her from the corner of his eyes, trying to see how she reacted. After a long moment, she lifted her hand to wipe her eyes, and continued weeding. With a small smile, Matthew resumed weeding, as well.

Now it was up to Eleanor and God.

Chapter Eighteen

"I'll be gone for a couple of weeks. I leave tomorrow," Matt said. It was Sunday afternoon, and he and Eleanor were slowly walking from church to the Jessups' home. Lucas and Susannah had gone on ahead, leaving them to themselves.

"Oh?" Eleanor looked sideways at him.

"Heading over to Kansas City again. Going to meet a man there about a herd he wants to sell. It's a big place in the cattle trade, Kansas City."

"So you'll be back around the fourteenth?" Eleanor asked. She was surprised to find how quickly she tried to calculate the exact date of his return.

"The fifteenth. I figure I might as well take care of as much business as I can while I'm over there. Saves my having to go again any time soon."

Eleanor was silent for a moment. They had settled into a comfortable pattern, seeing each other on Sundays and once or twice throughout the week. She greatly disliked the idea of Matt being gone, even if it only meant she saw him a handful fewer hours.

"I was hoping," Matt said, clearing his throat, "that once I get back, you and I could try having a talk again."

Eleanor stopped in her tracks. They spent a great deal of time talking already, so there was really only one thing he could mean by that. She expected to find herself upset by the idea, or to at least feel guilty about it. To her surprise, she didn't feel upset or guilty. In fact, Eleanor found that she was delighted.

"I think I would like that." She nodded slowly as a brief smile came to her lips.

Matt didn't respond right away, but he did smile broadly. Finally, he looked over at her. "I reckon Susannah is going to be pleased."

Eleanor laughed. "I expect she will. Then she'll think of something else to pester us about."

"She wouldn't be Susannah if she didn't."

The couple walked in companionable silence until they reached the house, where Matt kissed the back of Eleanor's hand and bid her good day. Eleanor then found Susannah peering through the barely-open front door.

"I wasn't looking out the window!" she exclaimed as Eleanor opened the door the rest of the way.

"No, I suppose you weren't." Eleanor was in too good a mood to be much bothered by Susannah's nosiness.

"I take it that went well, then," Lucas said. Eleanor was surprised to see that he was waiting for her return, as well. "He mentioned he was planning to talk to you today."

"I think it went well," Eleanor said with a smile. "We agreed to talk things over once he gets back from Kansas City."

Susannah bounced over to Eleanor and gave her a tight hug.

"Ooh, I'm just so happy for you, Ellie. I knew this was going to work out," she said.

"You got lucky," Lucas said firmly, looking over at his wife.

Susannah rolled her eyes at him. "Don't ruin my fun," she said.

Eleanor settled into her favorite chair in the sitting room and took up her needlework. She'd never been quite so happy just to sit in one place and embellish pillowcases before. She would have been happy to go out into the yard and turn over another garden plot entirely by hand.

Matt had been right. It was time to move to the next chapter in her life.

Chapter Nineteen

Cigar smoke hung heavy in the air, dimming the already moody light, and the sound of glasses clinking mixed with the low murmur of men's voices. This was the Bull's Head, a favorite haunt of ranchers, both for pleasure and for business. The place was crowded, even early in the afternoon, with rich men and their lady friends eating lunch and drinking down their afternoon sustenance.

Cigars might have been the standard, but Matthew preferred his old whittled pipe. Sitting in a sleek, leather-upholstered booth, he puffed away quietly. He'd paired his steak with a glass of lemonade, despite whiskey being a more standard choice in a place like this.

He had to get on the train in a few hours, headed back to Colorado. It wasn't the time for a drink. Matthew wasn't fond of strong drink or the effect it could have on a man, anyway. He chose to keep his head clear at all times.

His companion clearly felt otherwise. Mason Stratford, owner of a massive stretch of land in Texas, and the man who has recently sold Matthew nearly a thousand head of cattle, was making his way through his steak with the assistance of a liberal amount of bourbon.

"You sure you won't have a drink, Connor?" he said, cheeks already ruddy.

"Now you know I'm not a drinker, Mason." Matthew looked at the man with a blank face.

"Not even a toast to our mutual prosperity? Cold, Connor, cold." Stratford shook his head.

"I'd rather not wind up like those fellows." Matt jerked his head toward a table nearby, where a quintet of young men sat, playing cards. They'd gone through more shots than Matt could easily count just in the time it took to order and receive lunch. They were the noisiest table in the room, loudly yammering at each other over their hands.

"Pff. You're no greenhorn. You're a man, you can hold your liquor."

"That may be, but I'd still prefer not to," Matthew said firmly. Stratford sighed and shrugged dramatically, giving him up as a lost cause.

"It's too bad you're headed back to the mountains so soon," he said, cutting through his beef. "You should stay a while longer and enjoy the pleasures of civilization."

"I've got to be getting back. I've got someone waiting for me." Truth be told Matthew would rather have been back in the clean, fresh Colorado air with Eleanor the whole time, but he wasn't going to say it to his friend.

"A woman, eh? It's about time you settled down. Though I suppose that means we'll be seeing even less of you 'round these parts."

"I might bring her over to the city every now and then," Matthew said, considering the matter for the first time. "If she wants to come with me."

"I'd like to meet her. She's a lucky lady, snagging Matthew Connor."

If she doesn't change her mind again, the lucky one is going to be me, Matthew thought with a wry smile.

The young men next to them exploded into raucous shouts, one person cheering his triumph, another angrily shouting that he had cheated, and the rest of them urging them on. The floor manager nervously skittered up, trying to shush them without actually drawing attention to himself.

"I don't know how young'uns like that get in here," Stratford said with distaste. "This is supposed to be a respectable establishment."

Matthew shrugged. "It's some rancher's son and his friends, no doubt." He would be happy to be out of this club and onto that train, the sooner the better.

The losing party of the card game jumped to his feet, swinging wildly across the table. The room stilled, everyone watching, and the winner shouted and started swinging back. The poor manager wrung his hands, then ran off to find his boss.

While he fled, it finally occurred to the fighters that they could reach each other if they left the table, and they began wrestling in the space next to their seats. Their companions hooted encouragement, stomping their feet.

Matthew leapt from the booth, grimacing with displeasure. While Hartford shouted in alarm, he pushed through the crowd to where the young men were fighting and grabbed each one by the scruff of the neck.

"Just what do you think you're doing?" he growled. The two men continued to swing at each other, ignoring the fact that they were now suspended in midair.

"Hold still, you card-counting son of a gun!" the loser shouted. "I'm going to beat you so bad you'll wish you were run down by a bull!" Rather than reply, his opponent kicked out, catching him in the shin.

"Hey!" Matthew gave them a shake. He was about to knock their heads together when a hand landed on his arm.

"Let 'em fight it out, old timer." It was one of men who'd been observing the game, a cigarette hanging from his lips. "I've got a hundred dollars riding that Chet'll knock a few of Ted's teeth out."

"You're just as bad as they are," Matthew said, disgusted.

"I said, let them fight it out." The man repeated his direction slower this time. He yanked Matthew back by the arm, forcing him to drop the two drunken fighters. Pulling his fist back, he aimed a punch at Matthew's face, but Matthew ducked and the blow struck a large rancher standing behind him.

The innocent bystander shouted angrily, and punched back. Then the rest of the young men involved in the card game joined the fight, and before anyone knew what was happening the bar had devolved into a flurry of feet and fists.

Matthew knew when to pull out of a fight. Looking around, he tried to find a way to sneak toward the wall, but there was a metallic glint in the corner of his vision. One of the card players had pulled a gun. Matthew lunged at him, trying to knock the pistol from his hand, but he was tripped up by the crowd. There was a loud bang, the acrid smell of gunpowder, and Matthew heard no more.

Chapter Twenty

The fifteenth of August came, and Eleanor put on her blue suit. Matt's train was supposed to arrive during the service, and he was supposed to come calling for her shortly after. She had never been happier to sit in a church pew, though she hardly heard one word out of ten that Pastor Judd said.

Eleanor was equally happy to sit in the buggy on the way home, watching the bustle of late summer roll by. Susannah watched her from the corner of her eye, smiling as broadly as if it was her own sweetheart returning that morning. Lucas merely rolled his eyes. Once they arrived home and the horses were unhitched, Eleanor sat herself in the parlor with some needlework to wait for Matthew.

The appointed time arrived, and Eleanor peeked expectantly out the window, but nobody was coming down the drive. It wasn't unheard of for trains to be late. In fact, it was more normal than the trains being on time. She didn't start getting worried until several hours had gone by, with no sign of Matt whatsoever.

Lucas, frowning, went into town around five. He returned while the ladies were preparing supper with the news that while the train had been on time, not a soul had seen hide nor hair of Matthew Connor. All they could do was share a worried look between them and go to bed. Eleanor knelt by her bedside, praying fervently that nothing terrible had happened.

There was no word from Matthew in the morning, either, and the ladies set about the day's work with an air of anxiety. Eleanor dusted the parlor and swept out the kitchen, then stepped out to look for new weeds in the garden. She was beginning to relax, letting her thoughts drift away in the soothing rhythm of plucking and pulling when Susannah called her from the front of the house.

Wiping her hands on her apron, Eleanor headed around to see her. Maybe Matthew had arrived. The thought put a spring in her step, and she practically bounced around the corner. She was certain he'd have a good explanation and maybe even a funny story to tell.

Lucas and Susannah were wait waiting for her, looking very worried. Eleanor looked between their faces, concern beginning to flood the pit of her stomach again.

"What's wrong?" she asked hesitantly. Susannah just turned to Lucas, letting him speak first for once.

"There's been some news from Kansas City," he said.

His usual gruff air had been replaced with gentleness, which only made Eleanor more nervous. He handed her a folded newspaper and she took it with chilled fingers.

"What?" she asked with a shaky voice she had no control over.

"There was a big fight in one of the clubs that cattlemen use to do business," Lucas continued.

Eleanor unfolded the newspaper and looked at the headline. The paper shook in her hands as she read it.

TWO DEAD IN DRAMATIC
BARROOM BRAWL

*More Than A Dozen Injured When Fighting Breaks Out
Elite Ranchers From Five States Caught In Crossfire*

Worry unfolded into cold, dread certainly in Eleanor's gut.

"He's dead, isn't he?" she said, her voice already rough.

"Let's not jump to conclusions," Susannah said, quickly plucking the paper from Eleanor's hands. "There's got to be more than one place in a big city like that where ranchers do business. Right, Lucas?" She turned to her husband with a nervous smile, seeking his reassurance. Instead, he shook his head.

"I've, um, heard it through the grapevine that Matt was most definitely caught up in that fight," he said slowly, clearly afraid of the effect of his words.

Eleanor took a shuddering gasp.

"I can't tell you exactly what happened because the details are still unclear. You know how stories grow when they get passed around, and this one's crossed two states. All I know for certain is that he was involved."

"Now, now, I still don't think we should just assume the worst." Susannah stroked Eleanor's shoulder soothingly, trying to calm her distraught friend. "I'm sure we'll see him by this afternoon, or if not Matt himself, he'll send a telegram. He's fine. You'll see."

Eleanor nodded, but hope was already fading in her heart.

Chapter Twenty-One

Days passed with no news of Matthew, and days quickly turned into weeks. Susannah watched Eleanor with sadness and guilt. She was the one who had introduced her to Matt and even if she never could have predicted the fight, it was technically Susannah's fault that Eleanor was facing the loss of another man from her life.

She kept up hope, talking cheerfully of his return until the moment Lucas quietly took her aside and told her to stop, for Eleanor's sake. Lucas himself kept out of the way. He didn't know what to say, and solved the problem by not saying anything at all.

Eleanor was simply resigned. She'd done this before. No amount of tears, no amount of hoping or wishing or praying would bring back the dead, and in her mind Matthew was dead. He wasn't coming back. No more than John or her baby were going to come back. Matt had taught her that himself. She might as well get used to it.

The bigger question was what she was going to do. Eleanor had no intention of going back to Boston. She'd rather go work in a saloon than do that. She couldn't live on the Jessups' hospitality forever. At the very least, she had to find some way of earning her keep. That way she could bring some money into the household, and pay for her room and board.

These thoughts combined with the cold, creeping pain of loss were enough to keep her from speaking much to those around her. Eleanor went through her days mechanically, the rituals of cooking and cleaning the only things she could cling to. For the first time in her life, she was even too wretched to pray. Her lips barely moved when she mumbled grace at supper time. And what was worse, she didn't even mean any of the words she uttered.

Lucas and Susannah watched her silence with alarm. She hadn't been chatty when she arrived, but as Eleanor's friendship with Matthew grew, she'd come out of her shell, like a late-blooming flower finally showing its full and beautiful colors. It had become normal for Lucas to come home in the evenings to loud laughter as the two women worked and fellowshipped together.

Now, she didn't say anything at all. Entire days could pass with Eleanor barely saying five words, to Susannah and Lucas combined. The couple had a lively, if hushed argument almost every night about what they should do; Susannah wanted to find a way to cheer her up, and Lucas insisted that Eleanor be given space. The end result was that they tried to let her relax, and avoided the subjects of cattle, Kansas City, and Matthew Connor entirely.

Unaware of her friend's worries, Eleanor found that she had very little to do. Susannah was trying to keep most of the chores to herself, which was hurting more than it was helping. Eleanor would have loved the opportunity to fill her mind with even the meanest of manual labor. When her hands were still, her thoughts kept wandering back to the idea of Matthew, getting on a train and never coming home.

At the moment, Susannah was out weeding in the kitchen garden, while Eleanor sat in the sitting room, mending an old shirt of Lucas's, having gone through every item of clothing in the house looking for tears when Susannah wasn't watching. There wasn't much to fix, but it was at least something.

Just as Eleanor was tying off her thread, there was a knock at the door. Eleanor looked around, but Lucas was out working, and Susannah wouldn't be able to hear from the back of the house. She was going to have to deal with whoever the visitor was. Eleanor sighed, setting aside the shirt.

She expected to find one of Lucas's acquaintances, either trying to find him or deliver a message. The person on the other side of the door was one of his acquaintances, just not one of the ones she was expecting. Matthew stood on the porch. He seemed even more surprised than Eleanor when she shrieked at the top of her lungs and threw her arms around his neck.

"Ellie?"

Matt didn't have time to get another word out, because Eleanor planted a kiss right on his lips. Susannah, hearing Eleanor's shout, came running around the side of the house, saw what was going on, and went running right back out of sight.

"Where have you been?" Eleanor demanded as soon as she pulled away. She was on the verge of tears, and had to sniff madly to stop her nose from running.

"Kansas City?" Matt looked befuddled, if befuddled in a pleased sort of way.

"For a month? You were supposed to be back on the fifteenth!" Eleanor wiped her eyes. She was going to be calm about this, if it was the last thing she did.

"Didn't you get my telegram?" Matt asked, frowning.

"No." Much to her embarrassment, Eleanor continued to snuffle. She was far too old to be crying openly like a child. "We didn't get any messages about anything, and then the newspapers said there was a fight at the club in Kansas City and that people died, and—"

"That's a bit of an exaggeration," Matt said gruffly. "Someone got shot, but nobody died."

"How was I supposed to know that?" Eleanor demanded. "You just never came back!"

"Well, I'm back now. Just got a little banged up." Matt pushed her away just enough to how her his arm, still wrapped thick bandages.

Eleanor gasped. She'd been so happy to see him she hadn't even noticed. "They made me stay at the hospital a while, 'till the bump on my head went down. Wanted me to stay longer, actually, but I wasn't having that. I knew you'd be waiting for me."

"I thought—we thought you must've died," Eleanor said. She was forced to wipe her eyes again. Matt's expression had already been gentle, but now it became outright tender.

"There, now," he said softly, putting his hand on her shoulder. "I'm fine, see? Give me time to get these bandages off and I'll be fit as a fiddle."

Eleanor nodded, taking a deep breath.

"I'm glad you're back," she said quietly.

"I am, too." Matt paused for a second. "But I'd be gladder if you married me."

Eleanor gave a sniffly laugh.

"I thought we already decided to do that," she said.

"Well, I was afraid you might change your mind again," Matthew said.

Eleanor shook her head violently. "I wouldn't dare. Not this time." Burrowing in under Matthew's bandaged arm, she hugged him tightly. "I'm too grateful for this second chance. Not everyone gets this lucky."

Matthew dipped his head and gave Eleanor the sweetest kiss she'd ever received. Swept up in the moment, she kissed him back with all the pent-up love and worry she'd kept in her heart for the past month.

"I think I'm going to like being married to a woman who will kiss me like that." Matthew beamed down at Eleanor with no shyness or hesitation.

Eleanor tried to quell the blush creeping up her neck to her cheeks. She was certain her husband-to-be would manage to make her blush time and again as they spent their lives together. She looked forward to every moment of it.

Epilogue

Susannah and Lucas drove their carriage over to the Connor ranch. A year had passed, and summer was already melting into fall. The house bustled with activity as ranch hands went back and forth, preparing to drive a small herd to Denver for shipping. Lucas went to speak to Matthew, while Susannah let herself into the house.

To her surprise she found Eleanor and Mrs. Connor the elder downstairs, cheerily washing dishes in the kitchen. At the sight of her friend, Eleanor grabbed a towel and dried her hands.

"Should you be on your feet already?" Susannah asked, raising her eyebrows at Eleanor. Eleanor scoffed.

"Don't be silly. Everything went perfectly. You were there."

"Still. You should be taking easy," Susannah said.

"There's time for that later. Did I tell you I actually got letters from those brothers of mine the other day?" Eleanor said, leading Susannah across the house. "Apparently I'm worth acknowledging, now that I'm married to a ranch owner."

"That does sound like your brothers," Susannah said

drily. "How about your mother? Does she still bother you about coming west?"

That prompted a laugh and a grimace from Eleanor.

"I think I've finally convinced her to just stay in Boston. A little, um, assistance from Matt helped, I think. They won't have to worry about being evicted any time soon."

"That's probably for the best. Your family, his family, and your own family all in one place would be a bit much."

"Especially if our family keeps growing." They reached the bedroom, and tiptoed in.

A tiny baby, only a few days old, lay sleeping in a cradle. She was tucked up in a yellow blanket that Susannah had crocheted herself. Eleanor watched her friend's face carefully as she looked at the baby.

"We decided to name her Susannah. She would never have been born, if it weren't for you." Her face was hesitant, as though she was a little worried about how Susannah was going to react. Susannah just smiled and shook her head.

"That's sweet of you." It was a short sentence, but it said more than the sum of its words. Eleanor smiled in relief, continuing to talk.

"We haven't decided if she's going to be a Susie or an Anna yet," she said. "Obviously she can't just be Susannah. That'd too many Susannahs."

Susannah laughed, and smaller Susannah gurgled angrily at the noise.

"Now, now, don't fuss," Eleanor said, rocking the cradle back and forth.

Neither Susannah nor Eleanor wanted to admit it, but it was a bittersweet moment. They had used to share their childlessness, a bond neither of them wanted, but lived with, anyway. It was hard to see Eleanor sitting there, holding the happiness that Susannah could never achieve. In spite of all that, Susannah was feeling quite optimistic about the future.

Her success in marrying Eleanor off had given her a very good idea. Susannah couldn't help but smile widely as she watched the baby get rocked back to sleep. Oh, yes, she'd thought of something very good to occupy her time with.

Now she just had to convince Lucas to play along.

* * * * *

SPECIAL EXCERPT FROM

❧

LOVE INSPIRED
INSPIRATIONAL ROMANCE

*Can the new teacher in this Amish community help the
family next door without losing her heart?*

Read on for a sneak preview of
The Amish Teacher's Dilemma *by Patricia Davids,
available in March 2020 from Love Inspired.*

Clang, clang, clang.

The hammering outside her new schoolhouse grew
louder. Eva Coblentz moved to the window to locate
the source of the clatter. Across the road she saw a man
pounding on an ancient-looking piece of machinery with
steel wheels and a scoop-like nose on the front end.

When he had the sheet of metal shaped to fit the front
of the machine, he stood back to assess his work. He
knelt and hammered on the shovel-like nose three more
times. Satisfied, he gathered up his tools and started in
her direction.

She stepped back from the window. Was he coming to
the school? Why? Had he noticed her gawking? Perhaps
he only wanted to welcome the new teacher, although his
lack of a beard said he wasn't married.

She glanced around the room. Should she meet him
by the door? That seemed too eager. Her eyes settled on
the large desk at the front of the classroom. She should
look as if she was ready for the school year to start. A
professional attitude would put off any suggestion that
she was interested in meeting single men.

Eva hurried to the desk, pulled out the chair and sat down as the outside door opened. The chair tipped over backward, sending her flailing. Her head hit the wall with a painful thud as she slid to the floor. Stunned, she slowly opened her eyes to see the man leaning over the desk.

He had the most beautiful gray eyes she'd ever beheld. They were rimmed with thick, dark lashes in stark contrast to the mop of curly, dark red hair springing out from beneath his straw hat. Tiny sparks of light whirled around him.

"I'm Willis Gingrich. Local blacksmith." He squatted beside her. "Can you tell me your name?"

The warmth and strength of his hand on her skin sent a sizzle of awareness along her nerve endings. "I'm Eva Coblentz. I am the new teacher and I'm fine now."

Don't miss
The Amish Teacher's Dilemma
by USA TODAY *bestselling author Patricia Davids,*
available March 2020 wherever
Love Inspired books and ebooks are sold.

LoveInspired.com

LIEXP0220

*When Jed Dalloway started over, ranching a
mountain plot for his recluse boss is what saved him.
So when hometown girl April Reed offers a deal
to develop the land, Jed tells her no sale.
But his heart doesn't get the message...*

*Read on for a sneak preview of
the next book in* New York Times *bestselling author
Allison Leigh's Return to the Double C miniseries,*
A Promise to Keep.

"Don't look at me like that, April."

She raised her gaze to his. "Like what?"

His fingers tightened in her hair and her mouth ran dry.
She swallowed. Moistened her lips.

She wasn't sure if she moved first. Or if it was him.

But then his mouth was on hers and like everything
else about him, she felt engulfed by an inferno. Or maybe
the burning was coming from inside her.

There was no way to know.

No reason to care.

Her hands slid up the granite chest, behind his neck,
where his skin felt even hotter beneath her fingertips, and
slipped through his thick hair, which was not hot, but
instead felt cool and unexpectedly silky.

His arm around her tightened, his hand pressing her
closer while his kiss deepened. Consuming. Exhilarating.

Her head was whirling, sounds roaring.

It was only a kiss.

But she was melting.

She was flying.

And then she realized the sounds weren't just inside her head.

Someone was laying on a horn.

She jerked back, her gaze skittering over Jed's as they both turned to peer through the curtain of white light shining over them.

"Mind getting at least one of these vehicles out of the way?" The shout was male and obviously amused.

"Oh for cryin'—" She exhaled. "That's my uncle Matthew," she told Jed, pushing him away. "And I'm sorry to say, but we are probably never going to live this down."

Don't miss
A Promise to Keep *by Allison Leigh,*
available March 2020 wherever
Harlequin Special Edition books and ebooks are sold.

Harlequin.com

**HARLEQUIN**

Heartfelt or suspenseful, inspiring or passionate, Harlequin has your happily-ever-after.

With new books published every month, you are sure to find the satisfying escape you know you deserve.

HNEWS2020